SPEAKING OF THE
FANTASTIC II

OTHER BOOKS BY DARRELL SCHWEITZER

NOVELS

The Mask of the Sorcerer   The Shattered Goddess

The White Isle

COLLECTIONS AND STORY-CYCLES

Echoes of the Goddess   The Great World and the Small

Necromancies and Netherworlds (with Jason van Hollander)

Nightscapes   Refugees from an Imaginary Country

Sekenre: The Book of the Sorcerer   Tom Bedlam's Night Out

Transients   We Are All Legends

POETRY AND LIGHT VERSE

Groping Toward the Light

The Innsmouth Tabernacle Choir Hymnal

Non Compost Mentis   Poetica Dementia

Stop Me Before I Do It Again!   They Never Found the Head

NON-FICTION

The Dream Quest of H. P. Lovecraft

Lord Dunsany: A Bibliography (with S. T. Joshi)

On Writing Science Fiction: The Editors Strike Back

(with George Scithers and John M. Ford)

Pathways to Elfland: The Writings of Lord Dunsany

SF Voices (interviews)   SF Voices 1, 2, and 5 (interviews)

Speaking of Horror (interviews)   Windows of the Imagination

AS EDITOR

Another Round at the Spaceport Bar (with George Scithers)

Discovering H.P. Lovecraft   Exploring Fantasy Worlds

The Ghosts of the Heaviside Layer by Lord Dunsany

Discovering Modern Horror Fiction (2 vols)

Discovering Stephen King   Discovering Classic Horror Fiction

Discovering Classic Fantasy   The Neil Gaiman Reader

Speaking of the Fantastic II   The Thomas Ligotti Reade

Tales from the Spaceport Bar (with George Scithers)

SPEAKING OF THE FANTASTIC II

DARRELL SCHWEITZER

WILDSIDE PRESS

CONTENTS

INTRODUCTION: TIME-TRAVELING WITH A TAPE-RECORDER

If you've read the introduction to the first volume in this series, you can skip on ahead to the interviews. What I have to say here is pretty much what I said last time.

Here are a bunch of my old interviews with famous science-fiction and fantasy authors, presented exactly as originally published. No attempt has been made to update them. That means that when Peter Beagle hints at his forthcoming novel, he is describing what became *Tamsin* (1999). This is very much the point of reprinting old interviews. An interview, when published in a magazine like *Science Fiction Chronicle*, has an immediate, news value. But a book like this is archival. It is a form of time-travel. It lets you go back in time and read what Peter Beagle was thinking before he had completed *Tamsin*, or where Philip José Farmer was in his career in 1984. Three of the interviewees, Sheffield, Lafferty, and Walton, are, alas, no longer with us. What you read here comes close to being their last testaments.

If someone had gone back to interview Homer about the time he finished the *Iliad* and asked the obvious, news-of-the-moment question, "What are you working on next?" he might have replied, after a pause, "I'm thinking about a sequel. Don't know what I'll call it yet." That very hesitancy would be interesting. It would tell us that the *Odyssey* was not planned from the start. Any attempt to "update" the interview subsequently would destroy precisely this information and perspective.

So here you are, interviews ranging from 1983 to 2002. Here are voices from the past.

— Darrell Schweitzer
Philadelphia PA,
Nov 26, 2003

PETER S. BEAGLE

Q: I suppose one of the most striking things about your career, other than how fine the books are, is how few of them there are, over such a long period of time. Only three novels (and a couple of shorter works) in as many decades. How long has it been since *A Fine and Private Place?*

Beagle: *A Fine and Private Place* came out in 1960. Then my previous one—the one before the book that is coming out now—*The Folk of the Air*, came out in 1987. I got a letter from Robin McKinley the other day. She is the nearest thing I've got to a protegé. And Robin mentioned that as a slow writer herself, it was a great comfort for her to know I existed, because everybody else seemed to write faster than she did.

I write other things fast. I can write non-fiction fast, screen-plays fast, any bread-and-butter thing fast. Perhaps it is because I think differently about the novels, think in another gear if you like, that they come slowly.

Q: Is it because they're deeply personal?

Beagle: Perhaps it's because everything else I've always done to make a living. Writing is the one way I've ever known to put bread on the table. So I had to learn a lot of crafts of one kind or another. I had to learn to do them fast. But I never expected to make a living off the novels. So they come more slowly and they're altogether different from everything else I do.

Q: Once a novel is cooking, does it come quickly then, or is the actual act of writing slow, so that you might labor over two pages for a month and go on at that rate?

Beagle: Both. You have a good run, where the stuff is coming so fast you can't believe it's you, and then you have one of those stretches where, sometimes for no reason and sometimes for very good ones, you're just building those sentences word by word, and you just know you'll never get to the end of this chapter. As always, the trick is to make the ones that came easily and the ones that came hard look as if they both came at the same pace so that people tell you how it seems to have been born in one inevitable flow of creation. But I can overworry. I can sit for the longest damn time trying to find the exact word for something that doesn't quite exist.

Perhaps I write screenplays faster because I love to write dialogue. That's always come very easily for me. But a lot of my time is just taken up in rewriting. I begin *fussing*.

Q: What suddenly brought about *A Fine and Private Place*—if suddenly is the way to describe it? Why did you start then and there? I'd guess, for one thing, that you'd been reading a lot of Robert Nathan.

Beagle: I certainly had been. As far as I'm concerned—and although he always said it was nothing like it—*A Fine and Private Place* is, if not a dead steal, a direct descendant of a book of his called *One More Spring*, which was published in 1933, six years before I was born. I came across it in college. I wanted to do that.

As far as the genesis of *A Fine and Private Place* itself goes, I grew up a block and a half away from that cemetery. It was one of the few green places in the area, and my family and I and my friends and I used to go for walks there. I was going for a walk with my mother one afternoon, looking at an enormous mausoleum, and I can't remember which of us commented that if you could solve the food and water problems, you could probably live in one of these places. Well how would you be fed? Where would you get the food? I think I was the one who made the joke, "Well, like Elijah in the Bible, you get fed by a raven." And before we were out of the cemetery, I had the basic plot of the book.

Q: Presumably this manuscript was going on the market

around 1958 or 1959. It must have been fairly difficult to have such a work published at the time. Did the publishers have any idea what to do with it?

Beagle: Strangely enough, it was not at all difficult—and I know how unusual that was for the time. I was incredibly lucky in a lot of ways. I had been adopted, in a literary sense, by an old poet and his wife, Louis and Bryna Untermeyer, who came across me when I was about fifteen. When I was seventeen they handed me over to the woman who was my agent for twenty years until she died, Elizabeth Otis, who was also John Steinbeck's agent.

And Elizabeth simply sold the book. She had a bid on it before Viking from Doubleday and turned it down, thinking that Doubleday was not a fit place for a young writer of Elizabeth's standards. So she waited until Viking kicked in. And they did. I don't know how to describe it. It was another world, another attitude toward literature in some ways. I know how rare it was to have fantasy published and treated seriously in those days, but there!—the path was magically smoothed and I had no trouble at all, and I was taken, really, quite seriously for a first novelist. I didn't make a fortune off it or anything like it, but it's still in print.

Q: You had somehow gone up the literature track, rather than up the genre science-fiction/fantasy track. I am sure if the novel had been published by Ballantine Books in 1960, things would have been very different.

Beagle: You see, it's entirely arbitrary. Today I'm located—that book too—in the science fiction section of the bookstore. I understand why people who don't think of themselves as fantasy writers or children's book writers, or what-have-you, get very indignant at always finding themselves in that part of the bookstore, not in the literature section. There was a time, and it was not all that long ago, when things weren't quite as compartmentalized as that. Now it's so much a matter of packaging. If they don't know where to put you in the bookstore, you may never sell the book. You screw up the bookkeeping, you upset the sales reps. The one-of-a-kind writer, who is in neither this category nor that, like my wife, has a real problem. It's like when Avram Davidson was at the

University of California at Irvine. Nominally he was a member of the English department. They could never really decide whether he belonged there, or in the History department or the Philosophy department. This bugged them a good deal.

Q: Maybe your timing was just incredibly fortunate. One wonders what would have happened if, say, T. H. White had come along now.

Beagle: The odds are that he'd be in the fantasy section, but you never know. It's so arbitrary. It's what the editor persuades the company to market you as, and what people get into the habit of seeing you as. I'm thinking of this because I've been hearing from Robin McKinley, whose last book, *Deerskin* did a nose-dive and simply disappeared, because it was not what people expected from Robin McKinley. It's a fantasy, all right, but it's not what people look for from her. I think it's a marvelous book. It's a wonderful step forward for her, but the point is, she upset the packaging. I couldn't even find the book, and I looked.

Q: So now there is the problem of what people expect from Peter Beagle. Do you feel that you're in the shadow of *The Last Unicorn*?

Beagle: In some ways I'll probably always be. I'm resigned to it, but I'm damned if I'm ever going to do it again. I've tried very hard to make each book different from the last. It's a matter of pride and of interest as well. So far, I've been lucky. One way or another I've made a living all this time. I've raised children. I've made house payments. I don't know what's coming beyond the next check. I'm sure about the next one, but the one after that, I don't know. But I can't do things any differently.

It's not even a question of being courageous and taking a noble stand. My newest novel, *The Innkeeper's Song*, is very different from anything else I've ever done, because it wanted to be like that. I think it's the best I've ever done.

But I can remember that I came across a book by Edgar Pangborn which I had never read, a historical novel called *A Wilderness of Spring*, which was published in 1958. I thought it was a wonderful book. And I wrote to him and said, in effect, "I've known your stuff since I was a kid, but I have to say, honestly, I didn't know you were this good." Edgar wrote back and said that of all his books, that was the one that got blasted by the critics, disappeared completely, and is still hardest to find. As he remembered it, he got very drunk one night and sat up playing the piano, and the next day started writing another book.

Q: You seem to have gotten slightly more prolific in that the gap between *The Folk of the Air* and *The Innkeeper's Song* is not as great as the one between *The Folk of the Air* and *The Last Unicorn* [1968]. What's happened here?

Beagle: I'm not about to have an eighteen-year book gap again.

That's inexcusable. It wasn't a book gap. It was just a novel gap. I did other books in between there. But, no I would certainly like to be more prolific and I have other books that I want to get to in my life. I've always had to put them down to do something else to make money. But that's nothing to complain about. The miracle is that I do make some money. I just figure that as long as I keep up in the rude peasant health which, thank God, my rude peasant ancestors bequeathed me, I'll get to the books.

Q: Do books have their own time when they want to be written? This is, of course, only twenty-twenty hindsight, but *The Last Unicorn* would seem to be the sort of novel one would write in the mid-to-late '60s, as opposed to a novel one would write in, say, 1955.

Beagle: In fact I tried writing it in 1962, in the summer that I was staying with the friend with whom I traveled to California in *I See By My Outfit*. We were sharing a shack in Cheshire, Massachusetts. He was painted all day, and I was trying to work on a new book. The first few chapters of *The Last Unicorn* as people know it come from that summer of '62. But there was another eighty-five or so pages that just never went anywhere. I'd give a good deal to know where they did go, because I'd like to look at them now. But they vanished completely, and I just dropped the book for a couple of years. I came back to it around 1965, after *Outfit*, and completed it. I don't know that it particularly had anything to do with the time or with who I was then or what I was trying to do with the book. The first book, *A Fine and Private Place*, was an homage to Robert Nathan. *Unicorn* is very much an homage to T. H. White, Thurber, and Lord Dunsany certainly, and James Stephens, as well as Bob Nathan.

I think that perhaps what I like about the new book, *The Innkeeper's Song*, is that it isn't an homage to anybody. Whatever it is, it's its own self.

Q: What was *The Folk of the Air* an homage to, except perhaps Berkeley, California? I had not seen Berkeley when I read the book, but later, when I came to the Bay Area for the first time, it all fit.

Beagle: I tend to go back and forth between imaginary worlds, fairy-tale worlds, and the contemporary world. *A Fine and Private Place* did take place in the world I knew. *The Last Unicorn* is a fairy tale. *The Folk of the Air* took place in California. I am most pleased that you recognized it as Berkeley, because I never assumed it would be. Some people do that beautifully, and I wasn't at all sure if I were turning Berkeley into something unrecognizable.

The new book, *Innkeeper*, is set in an imaginary world, and the book I am beginning to work on now is a ghost story and set in our time, in the '90s. So I seem to go back and forth, in a pattern I wasn't aware of until recently.

Q: Could you say something more about *The Innkeeper's Song*? You may be more prolific than before, but a new Peter Beagle book is still infrequent enough to be news.

Beagle: Briefly, I love to write songs. *Innkeeper* comes out of a song I wrote one evening, called just that, "The Innkeeper's Song." For some reason the fit seized me, to take the figure of an innkeeper—who is usually a fat mein host or a skinny villain, letting the assassins in while you sleep—and these women in the song, black and brown and white, show up at his inn one night. The black one carries what he realizes is a sword-cane and walks rather like a sailor. The brown one has a pet fox that she takes with her, and the white one has a beautiful emerald ring on her finger. They simply take over his room. They sing, they laugh, they carry on, they fight, they cry, they sing again, they eat their way through his cheese and mutton; they call down for more wine—and ask him to send up the stable boy. In the morning they leave, and he's not sure who they were, what hit him, what their mission was or where they're going. The only thing he's really sure of is he'll have to get a new stable boy.

So I left it at that. It was one night's work, and I began only a few years later thinking of it as a novel. It's told from the point of new of all the people in the song and many who aren't. The innkeeper himself says that although the song has his name on it, he never wrote it. He's not a songwriter; he's an innkeeper. He gripes that the damn fox is in the song too. He always hated that fox.

I loved being all these different people. It was one of the nicest experiences I've had as a writer, because I've never used the "I" point-of-view in fiction. For me this was pure luxury. The next one is also told from a first-person point-of-view, but only one. I had been the omniscient author for so long that this is a real vacation from knowing every side to a story.

Q: It's odd that you'd never actually done first-person before.

Beagle: Most writers seem to start out that way. But surely there are delights in both methods. The omniscient author gets to meet more people. One reason I like doing first-person is that I love theater and I'm comfortable with actors—we have some in the family—and I like being other people. The real wonder for me of writing fiction is that you don't have to be stuck with the person you are all the time. Joyce Cary, who is one of my favorite writers, had an incredible gift for writing from the point of view of somebody he wasn't. His trilogy, *Herself Surprised, To Be a Pilgrim,* and *The Horse's Mouth*, is told from the viewpoints of three people who have crossed each other's paths to one degree of another over forty years. They aren't at all alike, and how Cary could be all these people and feel and think like them is an absolute joy and a wonder to me to this day; because they aren't Joyce Cary, at least not obviously. There's always that connection, Heaven knows, between you and the character. There's always that corner where you blend and blur. But if ever I'm talking about the things you can do with first person, I always use Cary as an example.

Q: Aside from being people you aren't, how about being people you are? How much autobiography is in your novels?

Beagle: Really not a whole lot. In terms of thoughts, feelings, undoubtedly, but I very rarely use people I've known directly in my books, for instance. There's an element here, a turn of speech there, and that's all. I think I don't like most fiction that tends to be heavily autobiographical. There are always exceptions, but I'm very reticent, and I have an air of not being reticent. I hide and mask things very well. It's not an act. When I was in therapy in Seattle getting acquainted with my therapist, who was a good man, he asked, "Well, tell me something about yourself. Do you have any hobbies? Do you collect things?" I told him, "I collect masks and boxes. You want to make something of it?" And we both laughed. But I do. I love masks. I love personae. I love, again, actors. To me it's so much more fun to live somebody else's autobiography in fiction than my own. Robert Nathan began writing an autobiography once. I have the partially completed manuscript. He got up to about 1944 and gave it up. As he said to me at the time, "What's the point of it. I just don't like going back through and making all those mistakes again." I understand fully. My own life really doesn't interest me to write about, except for the odd story or funny one-liner. But I do like to invent and borrow and synthesize lives.

Q: How well and how long did you know Robert Nathan? Was he in any sense a mentor?

Beagle: I read his work very much in high school and college. My mother remembers me calling her from college to tell her about this guy I'd been reading a lot of, and saying, "I want to write like that." Of course I'd been saying that about different writers since I was a kid, from Saroyan to Steinbeck on up. But Nathan stuck. We were introduced by a mutual friend around '64 or '65, and I was friends with him for the last twenty years of his life. He lived to be ninety-one. I always saw him when I was in Los Angeles. We wrote a great many letters to each other. I'm not sure if he was a mentor or not. He said to me once in utter candor, "I think you work gets better as it moves away from mine." But from him I learned a great deal about the life of a person who can't not be a writer and what you do when people think you died in 1950 and you still have to write. He was a bitter man in a lot of ways, and with good reasons. He was also funny. He'd lived a life that he didn't think was interesting, but

I though was. Some of the nicest moments I like to remember were spent at his house. I'm still in touch with his widow, the actress Anna Lee. She's still on *General Hospital*, although she's just turned eighty. And, I miss him. I hadn't realized that until I was talking about him fairly recently. It struck me that it's been eight years, and I do miss him. I'd still like to get another letter from him. Like Avram [Davidson], he wrote very funny letters.

Q: He's somebody whose work needs a bit of championing, I think. Virtually all of his work is forgotten. Most fantasy readers have no idea who he was. For some reason he never got discovered by the fantasy field.

Beagle: He got forgotten by the mainstream field and never discovered by the fantasy field. The only book of his that anyone is likely to know now is *Portrait of Jennie*. We talked about that because he said that *The Last Unicorn* would likely dominate everything I did and I'd have to live with it. He said, "There were times I'd just get furious about *Portrait of Jennie*, because I know I wrote a number of books that were better than that. Nobody knows them and they never will. And there are other times when I think, 'How can I hate Jennie?' So many wonderful things happened to me because of that book. Better that they should have happened for whatever reason, than never to have happened at all."

I've read Robert Nathan's work aloud at gatherings when I was reading from other people. I remember doing an evening's worth of readings from people's work that meant something to me. I like to think that eventually he will be reprinted and rediscovered. But it's very difficult to be immortal if you're not in print. The greatest thing that Hemmings and Condell did for Shakespeare was to keep him in print. Books disappear. They tear off the covers and pulp them.

Q: I suppose your career will be dominated by *The Last Unicorn*. But, had you not written *The Last Unicorn*, would another book of yours have achieved that purpose, or would you merely be an obscure author today?

Beagle: I simply don't know. There are too many "ifs" involved in that. The thing you have to do is, on the one hand, keep your head down and do your work, and then—and this is the hardest thing—to train yourself to live with rejection. My line is, "Hell, I've been thrown out of better joints than this." You must develop at all costs a kind of arrogance—if that's the word—which keeps you believing somehow that what you are doing will have hearers, will find someone, and is important, and you know how to do it. Words to live by. A story I tell a lot of people has to do with Ethel Merman on stage, in the wings on opening night, being asked if she wasn't scared when she thought how many celebrities were in the audience. Merman's answer, apparently, was, "F—'em. If they could do what I do, they'd be up here." And if I could stitch that into a sampler, I would, because it's very important to believe that, even if it's not true.

Q: But then, you actually have something to back it up with. There are people out there who have all the arrogance, and nothing to deliver.

Beagle: That's given, certainly. I think it was Dizzy Dean who said in all innocence, when accused of bragging about his pitching, "It ain't bragging if you can do it." And he could. I'm not sure Ernest Hemingway ever said anything else really wise, but he did say one thing when dealing with critics. He said, "If you believe them when they tell you you're good, you believe them when they tell you you're bad." It is important to develop this kind of tunnel-vision, arrogance—call it what you will—that says, "I have to do this and it doesn't matter that it's entirely insignificant in the cosmic order of things." I have to do this, and it's something that I can do that nobody else is, because if somebody else was doing it, I would read it. You have to believe that, whether or not you can deliver. In the end, that's such a subjective matter anyway. But you have to believe it.

Q: All of your fiction is fantasy. What is the special appeal of fantasy for you? Why isn't there, in the midst of all this fantasy, a detective novel or a realistic novel about life in California or something like that?

Beagle: I would love to write a detective novel. I hope to do that before I die.

I have an historical novel I'd like to do. But the fact is that fantasy is a way I think. Even if I wrote a "mainstream realistic" novel, the fact that I am a fantasy writer would still inform it somehow. Peter Dickinson says, "I am a science-fiction writer if I never write a word of science fiction, and I hardly ever have. I write all kinds of stuff, not just science fiction, but I approach everything like a science-fiction writer." He knows what he means a bit better than I do, but I know that I approach everything, including total realism, like a fantasy writer. It's just how I am.

Q: Is it possible to define this approach?

Beagle: I don't think so. It doesn't have to do with monsters or alien forms of life. I'm not even sure it has to do with language. It's just a way of seeing things, perhaps of being a bit more aware of the things that go on just beyond the corner of your eye, of a feeling that the laws of the cosmos operate as they should when you're watching them; but on alternate Thursdays, who knows? Perhaps it's just a child's awareness that a lot more is possible than adults tell you. I think most kids have this. When I was little I firmly believed that everything was alive, whether it moved or not. In some way, maybe that's it. Maybe I still do.

Q: How much of fantasy is deliberate artifice, with the fantastic elements deliberately made up? This is where I would draw the line between occult fiction and fantasy fiction. If you believe it's true, that's occult fiction. If you're aware you're making it up, that's fantasy.

Beagle: I know I'm making it up, but the paradox is that sometimes you make it up so well that it turns out true. I don't know how else to describe it. I once had someone come up to me, an editor I knew, who had read part of *The Folk of the Air*, which mentions a particular character, and said, "I didn't know you knew ___" and he named a friend of his, whom of course I had never heard of. He was absolutely convinced that I knew that particular person. I believe very greatly in the power of making things up. I'm glad you mentioned that.

Q: In a sense, fantasy may be an attempt to improve on reality.

Beagle: It's to get at reality, to get at some underlying reality. To me, paradoxically, fantasy seems to be the only way of approaching the truth.

Q: To conclude, can you talk a little bit about the book you've just started—or is that dangerous?

Beagle: I don't want to talk too much, because you wind the spring down. I'll just say that it is a ghost story, though not like *A Fine and Private Place*. It does take place in the modern world, part of it in the United States and the bulk of it in England, where I haven't been for a long time. I need to go back to England, to get the smell of things, if you like. The story is told from the point of view of a girl of twelve or thirteen, which, for all I know, will mean the tendency will be to market it in a different category, as a young adult novel. I hope not, simply because there's a question of money. Young adult means less money. But, there are ghosts in it, though it isn't *A Fine and Private Place*. There are two ghosts, and there are night-creatures of English folklore. One thing I've realized, again, thinking about Robin McKinley's books after I got her letter—one thing we have in common is that there is always an animal in our stories somewhere. In this particular one there is the girl's cat, whose name is Mister Cat. She's always called him that, just Mister Cat. And there is a ghost cat, and her name is Miss Sophia Brown. That's as much as I feel like going into.

Q: Thank you, Peter.

OCTAVIA BUTLER

[Note: This interview was done at Eeriecon, in Niagara Falls, NY, April 21, 2002, where Octavia and I were both guests of honor, and was conducted in front of the convention as her guest-of-honor presentation.—D.S.]

Q: To sort out your awards . . .

Butler: I won a Nebula for "Bloodchild" and for *The Parable of the Sower,* and I won a Hugo for "Bloodchild" and "Speech Sounds."

Q: So you have an impressively-stocked mantelpiece already.

Butler: I wish I had a mantel. It would be nice to put things up there. I just finally bought a house and it has no mantel. But it's funny to get three awards for my short stories when I'm essentially a novelist.

Q: But you must have started short.

Butler: I started writing short stories when I was very young. I started trying to sell them when I was thirteen. Fortunately nobody wanted to buy them. By the time I was able to sell anything, the first two things I sold were short stories, but thereafter I sold novels. Thereafter being five years later. I was one of the early Clarionites. I went to Clarion 1970. I sold two short stories, my very first sales, and I was so happy because then I knew I was a writer, and I would go home and write things, and people would buy them, and I'd be set for life. And it really hurt me when I didn't sell another word for five years.

Q: And one of those early stories was in *The Last Dangerous Visions* . . .

Butler: That is the one that you'll never see. Everybody knows about *The Last Dangerous Visions,* I assume.

Q: It's sort of the Flying Dutchman of science fiction.

Butler: It's like, for a while I sort of hoped it would come out. Now, I'm really glad it didn't. Who wants their student work to come out twenty, twenty-five years later?

Q: You mentioned in the afterword to your story-collection, *Bloodchild,* that when you were a kid and you were trying to write, your elder relatives were telling you, "Oh nonsense. You can't do *this* . . ."

Butler: It's kind of hard to convince people who came through the Depression the hard way that you're going to earn a living telling stories. What they're telling you is, "Grow up. Get a nice job with a salary and a pension." They couldn't figure out why I didn't think this was a good idea. I had a lot of jobs and I got to write about some of them later in *Kindred.* I gave them to my character. This is what writers do with their troubles and the unpleasantnesses of life. We give them to our characters. It makes them worthwhile.

I quit all those jobs. I think the very last one after I'd sold three novels and still had to do horrible little jobs was working in a hospital laundry in August. Thoroughly unpleasant.

Q: In the Afterword to *Bloodchild* you talk about the need for persistence—

Butler: I'd done an essay on habits, good habits for would-be writers to establish. I said the most important one is persistence. That is also what I say when I am asked what talent I think is most important for a writer: just to keep at it until you finally do have some success. One of my favorite teachers, Harlan Ellison, used to say, "If anything can stop you from being a writer, don't be one." I suspect that goes without saying. There are so many things out there that are out to stop you. It's not a conspiracy or anything, but it's just so difficult to become a writer and live on your writing. So persistence is a good . . . talent may not be the right word, a good habit to develop.

Q: One thing I wanted to ask you about from the same

Afterword is where you said that persistence is more important than talent. I have certainly know wannabes who had every conceivable writerly virtue except talent. I know somebody who is a Clarion graduate, too, who has been beating his head against the wall for the past twenty-five years. He's never sold a word. I think he simply doesn't have it.

Butler: There may be another skill that he doesn't have, and that's learning from his mistakes. I remember having a Clarion student who told me she'd written something like eight unpublished novels. The problem was, she was good, but she would refuse to learn from her mistakes. She would just trash whatever it was and start again on something else. Your friend might be doing that.

I justify saying that talent may be unimportant by suggesting that students go read the books on the Bestseller List and see who else doesn't have any talent.

Q: Except for the celebrities who have the books ghosted for them, surely any published writer has to have a certain narrative ability.

Butler: You'd think so, wouldn't you? I've read some unbelievably poorly-written stuff and I finally realized that good writing is just not a requirement, unfortunately.

Q: Let me bounce something off you. I have the Theory of Audience Starvation, which would account for a writer as bad as, say, James Femimore Cooper, who, as you know, was just dreadful in every conceivable way, *but he was writing about what the audience wanted to read about,* which is to say the American frontier. If he had been writing conventional romances, set in Europe, he wouldn't have been publishable.

Butler: I agree. I have been reading romances recently. [Laughs.] Not the kind you're talking about, but I just wanted to see what's out there and why are people buying it. I realized that there is absolutely nothing in the book that is of any quality at all *except* the romance.

Q: It's got to have something the readers want. I'd suggest that if Tom Clancy wrote westerns, we'd never have heard of him. He came along at the time when the audience wanted technothrillers and he was competent enough to make himself intelligible.

Butler: He's also a decent storyteller, and that's important. I think the most important thing a writer can do is tell a good story. If you don't do that, whatever else you do is liable not to be noticed.

Q: If you just write beautifully textured prose and there is no story, people will go to sleep after a while.

Butler: To me, that is what writer's block is. You're writing really well. You're getting nowhere. Hundreds of pages go by. Nothing much happens. To me, that's writer's block. I know, because I've been in the throes of one for a while, and I finally decided to quit what I was doing and write a non-fiction piece.

Q: Is that the unconscious telling you that the novel you're writing isn't ready yet?

Butler: Either that it isn't ready yet, or that it just isn't a novel. There's always that. I have an unpublished novel called *Blindsight,* which no one will ever see, except those few people who work for a certain publisher. It is no good because it doesn't go anywhere. I have a character and he does stuff, and that's pretty much it. I've got this blind psychic and he does stuff. Some of it is interesting stuff, but it doesn't really get anywhere in particular.

Q: Do you think you can come back to it someday and find the plot?

Butler: No. Some things just should be let alone, I think. I rewrote it many times. This was on a manual typewriter. It was before computers. I rewrote it many times, and I'm done with it.

Q: Of course if you become *really* famous, after you're dead they'll either publish it as a fragment or farm it out to somebody.

Butler: I hope not. It's what I said. It's not really worth publishing. I realize that someone might want to do it just for money. My heir, the person who will control things after I'm dead might very well do it, but I'll haunt her if she does.

Q: This has happened to any number of other writers. I recall how E. Hoffmann Price, in old age, burned certain things in self-defense.

Butler: I can't do it. I find it very difficult to get rid of things. I am a natural packrat. My mother gave me this packrat gene. It just means that when I'm dead there'll be so much junk that my cousin, who is my heir, will be just swimming in it. After a while she'll probably just give up and burn it all. Which won't be a bad thing.

Q: Or she could bring in vast quantities of scholars who will catalogue it all.

Butler: She doesn't have the patience.

Q: Is there a university already collecting your papers?

Butler: Actually there is. I'm willing them, not to a university, but to the Huntingdon Library because they asked for them and because Pasadena is my home town. So whatever I put together and mark will go to them.

Q: Let's talk about the sciences you find interesting. A lot of your stories that I've read have been based on biology, "Bloodchild," for instance. So, what attracts you to speculative biology?

Butler: No idea. I just follow my interests, and this has been an interest of mine for quite a long time. When I was in college I majored in quite a number of things for about five minutes each, and one of them was anthropology. I had the idea that I was going to be interested in cultural anthropology. Then I took that physical anthropology class and realized that what I was really interested in was evolutionary biology. I'm not interested in it enough to actually go and do something with it, but enough to read about and write about. I can't tell you why. It's just true.

I do follow my interests. If something attracts me, especially if it won't let me alone, I am happy to write about it.

Writers go through these periods of, you've got all these ideas and you're writing them, and then, after a while, you've written them, and you're refilling the well. I think I'm going through a period of refilling the well.

Q: Sprague de Camp used to say that as he got older, he had fewer ideas and so wrote more about them.

Butler: When I got the idea for *Patternmaster,* I was twelve years old. When I got the idea for *Mind of my Mind,* I was fifteen. I was nineteen when I got the idea for *Survivor,* which you won't see—and I hope you haven't already seen it, because it's bad—

Q: Is that the one you once described as your *Star Trek* novel?

Butler: Yeah, because the human beings go off to another world and immediately begin intermarrying with the natives, something that happens all the time on *Star Trek*.

Q: And they all wear jumpsuits and the landscape looks like southern California . . . and then there's a shopping mall, right?

Butler: Not quite, but it's got its problems. But the reason I'm saying all this is that I got these ideas early on. I got the idea for *Kindred* while I was in college. This meant that when I finally began to sell, years later, I had all these ideas and I was working on them. They spawned other ideas. Then after a while, I'd written all that, and then I had to look around and see what else I wanted to do. That's when I wrote my *Xenogenesis* novels. I didn't know at first that there would be three of them, but I finally figured it out, three novels. It kind of worked out nicely. Then I got to the *Parable* books, and that was more diffi-cult, because, well, they weren't something I'd lived with for a long time. It took me a while to get to the point of being able to write them. I had to get to know these characters. I had to get to know their world.

I guess that's what I'm doing right now. I have several ideas. I have been writing at them. I've been writing several hundred pages of non-novel, and that's why I'm doing the non-fiction right now. It doesn't require me to be inspired, or anything else. It just requires me to do the research.

Q: What's the non-fiction?

Butler: It's a name book, which is all I want to say about it, and it's *not* a name dictionary. I'll say that. It's something I used to wish I had, and never found.

Q: Isn't that also the way one writes novel?

Butler: In a sense, yes. When I started writing, one of the things I wanted to do was write myself in, because I was reading a lot of science fiction. I used to have a teacher who said, "Young science fiction writers read way too much science fiction." It was pretty much all I was reading. And I couldn't find me in there, so I wrote myself in.

Q: Did you have any perception at that time, as others have reported, that science fiction was supposed to be a man's game?

Butler: Not that. The nice thing about being an only child and a hermit is that I could imagine myself in all kinds of situations, and there was no one around to tell me I was being an idiot. And when my family finally did tell me I was an idiot, I didn't believe them, because by then I didn't believe them about much of anything.

Q: How did they react when you started publishing books?

Butler: They weren't impressed until I was able to quit that laundry job. No matter how many books you're publishing, if you're working at a hospital laundry, something's wrong . . . although I remember another writer and I corresponding, and he had dropped out. I said, "Why haven't I seen more from you?" He said, "Well, I didn't make anything on my first three books." My comment was, "Who makes anything on their first three books?"

I remember that the time I quit that laundry job, it was to go to a Worldcon in Phoenix. Figure back to when that was. [1978—D.S.] I should have gotten more jobs, but I decided I was going to try to live as frugally as possible, and at that time you really could live very frugally. My rent was a hundred dollars a month. So if you were content not to drive, and if you were content to wear the same clothes that you'd been getting along on for a long time . . . and there were other ways of not spending lots of money. I didn't eat potatoes for years after that.

I decided that I was going to live off the writing, somehow. My next novel was *Kindred,* which I didn't want to sell to Doubleday, because I got the same amount for the first three Doubleday books, and that same amount was $1750.00. Even then, that wasn't a lot of money. So I wanted to get more for *Kindred,* which I felt really was my best work to that time. And I wound up shopping it all over the place, and I ended up taking it back to Doubleday. No one else wanted to take a chance on it, because nobody knew what it was. It didn't quite qualify as science fiction. It didn't qualify as anything else, really. They didn't know what it was, so they didn't want it, and so I wound up in the Doubleday trade department. I got a little more money and used it to hire myself a publicist, and I began to do a bit better.

Q: Now you're doing a lot better, it would seem. Your books are in a lot of stores, unlike those Doubleday books, which doubtless disappeared instantly and became fabulous collector's items.

Butler: Yes. People pay a lot of money for them now. Oh well . . . [Laughs.] I still have some of them, so, who knows? They're kind of part of my retirement.

Q: What is the genesis of the two *Parable* books? These are a bit of a departure—

Butler: No, they're not, really. They're another case of me trying to fix the world, trying to fix the human species. We seem so likely to destroy ourselves. We work so hard at doing things which will harm us. I figure that if we ever do die out as a species, it will be because of something we did, as opposed to the asteroid striking, or something.

I keep trying to find ways to fix us. In the *Xenogenesis* books, genetic engineering. In the earlier books, mental abilities, telepathy, that kind of thing. In the *Parable* books, I made a rule: no aliens, no powers, no humanity-altering genetic engineering, just what we've got to work with. So people have to find a way, using the tools we've got. The tool my character chooses is religion. It's not really different; it's just going at the same thing in a different way.

Q: I've heard you speak elsewhere and describe gloomy prognostications for the future, what you refer to as "The Burn." Could you describe that?

Butler: That's just something I was working on for the *Parable* books. It was renamed the "Apocalypse," then shortened to the "Pox." "The Pox" is the nasty part of history that happens as a result of all the problems that we're neglecting now, from illiteracy to drugs to global warming, that are likely to give us trouble in the future just *because* we're ignoring them now. Today's troubles that grow up into tomorrow's disasters. Unfortunately, a lot of them mature at the same time. That's "The Pox." It's supposed to be something that we're already working on. It's already happening now. It comes to maturity in the 2020's.

Q: Here we are in Niagara Falls in mid-April and it's eighty degrees out. It was ninety in Philadelphia.

Butler: We can enjoy it . . .

Q: We can, but when I was a kid, we had Spring.

Butler: I remember being on a television program in Chicago where highschool children were allowed to ask questions, and somebody got me talking about global warming. And the other person on the program said, "It's nothing really to worry about."

I asked, "How can you say that?"

He said that getting warmer is just not that much of a problem. It's been warmer than we're likely to get. Why worry about it?

Of course it has, but not while we were around with all our cities built on coastlines. I think that that attitude, of "it's nothing to worry about," and the tendency to treat each incident that might relate to global warming as a separate incident is one of the things that is liable to get us to something very like The Pox.

Q: You could buy beachfront property five hundred miles inland from New Orleans . . .

Butler: I've just moved from southern California to Seattle. In 1999, I did that. I think I believe a little bit of what I've been saying.

Q: Do you think that writing novels about this has much impact?

Butler: Not now, no. Not enough people are suffering. I do think novels and movies and TV shows had an impact on whether or not we had that thermonuclear war. I think novels and films matter when people begin to get frightened, because then novels help them to imagine possibilities, that maybe they don't want to imagine, but they need to.

Q: There's a great Ray Bradbury line, that the purpose of science fiction is not to predict the future, but to prevent it.

Butler: Perhaps to give warning. There's an old idea that science fiction has the three categories, the "What If," "If Only," and "If This Goes On." The *Parable* books are definitely an "If This Goes On story."

Q: If we are to be a little more pessimistic, I would think that a religion that would come out of a crisis like The Burn would be a really militant, nasty one.

Butler: It could be. In fact, a nasty one does come out. But there's also my characters' religion. I grew up, had my adolescence during the space-race. I used to get up at three or four in the morning and watch the space-shots go. It seemed to me that

that was our way of having that nuclear war without having it. We were able to get the technological boost. We were able to compete with our enemies, and we were able not to kill a good portion of the human species in the process. I thought about that, when I created Earthseed, the religion of my character. I thought, what might she propose as a goal that might be worth going after, but that wouldn't involve wiping out a good portion of humanity? What I thought of was the idea of going to the stars. It is such a huge, difficult, long-term family of projects that it just might hold our attention, give us the boost we need, especially when it comes as a religious mandate. It could also cause a lot of trouble. It probably would, considering that we human beings are good at finding things to fight about, making trouble where it isn't necessary. But I had my character persist and manage to at least get people started.

Q: Are you optimistic or pessimistic toward the future? Utopia, disaster, or do we just somehow muddle through?

Butler: I don't know. The problem is that we're really good at responding to crises, but we're really bad at long-term planning, especially when it requires that we stop doing something that we really enjoy doing, like burning fossil fuels. Probably we will muddle through for a while, but sooner or later we'll push the environment too far. We'll do something that we won't be able to recover from.

Q: Indeed, if we ever did have that thermonuclear war, it might not be possible to build civilization again, because, among other things, all the easily obtainable fuel and metals have already been mined out and you have to have high technology to extract what's left.

Butler: Or we might have to do something else. Our inventiveness is not something that I have a problem with. It is our tendency not to plan far enough ahead. We might see the cliff. I don't drive. I am one of the few people I know who lived in Los Angeles for most of my life who doesn't drive. The reason I don't drive is that I'm a bit dyslexic. I have fairly quick reactions, but they're strange. When I was learning to drive, my teacher had me on a little mountain road, a two-lane road where you really had to squeeze past another car, and I was headed out on this little windy road, and I realized that I had to turn. Left and right mean nothing to me. You can say, "Go left," and if my life depends on it, I'm liable to go right. So the teacher wanted me to go a certain way, and it was obvious that I should because the other way was off a cliff. Well, I didn't process what he said and I went the wrong way. If there had not been dual controls on the car, I wouldn't be here.

I think, sometimes, there is a problem like that with the human species. We might see the right way, but we don't do it, not because we're dyslexic, but because we just find it more comfortable or more financially rewarding to go the wrong way, at least as long as we can.

Question from the audience: Are you going to write more of the *Parable* books?

Butler: Not with the same main character, because she's dead. I had the idea of following two or four groups who leave. There's a verse in the character's religion that says, "God is teacher, trickster, chaos, clay." I was going to do *The Parable of the Trickster, The Parable of the Teacher, The Parable of Chaos,* and *The Parable of Clay.* It didn't work out. I still might do them, but I'm not doing them now.

As a matter of fact the fiction I am working or now, or that I was working on before I went to the non-fiction book, is an odd fantasy that I suddenly came up with because I used to know a very interesting lady that I've never been able to use in a story before. She's found her way into this one.

Q: It sounds like you've been hit by lightning several times during your career, and have spent the rest of your life writing that out.

Butler: Everybody is.

Q: Everybody is, but most people don't recognize it and do anything with it.

Butler: It's more lighting, really. I wait until there's something that won't let me alone. I don't always wait. Sometimes I dive right in too quickly. But, best case, I wait until something won't let me alone, either because I agree, or I disagree with it, or because it fascinates me.

Q: What I mean by being hit by lightning is a case like Bram Stoker. He spent most of his life as a theatrical manager, but he still cranked out a number of routine books. He got hit by lightning once, and wrote *Dracula,* and nothing else he did mattered.

Butler: I am a little bothered by your putting it that way. I understand what you mean. It's one of the things that I try to keep young writers from thinking, that you have to wait, that it's all luck, lightning will strike and then you'll have a wonderful bestseller. So I think it's like the old idea that fortune favors the prepared mind. If you've developed the habit of paying attention to the things that happen around you and to you, then, yeah, you'll get hit by lightning.

Q: I think that you should tell the young writers to write up every story they feel like writing, because you only know in retrospect and possibly years later, if you were ever hit by lightning.

Butler: I don't think so. You'd waste an awful lot of time writing crap.

Q: True, but to use the example of Stoker, did he know that *Dracula* was head and shoulders above everything else he ever wrote, when he wrote it, or did he only discover this long afterwards?

Butler: On the other hand, did he write every thought he had?

Q: He probably didn't have time to. He had a very busy life.

Question from audience: Classical music is classic music because it has survived beyond its marketing age. The stuff that you don't hear anymore, maybe you don't hear because it wasn't so good—

Butler: Maybe it just didn't have the necessary PR.

Fan: Maybe the rest of Bram Stoker's books weren't very good.

Butler: But I don't think this is something you should worry about. I remember being on a panel at a science fiction convention years ago, and one of the questions put to us was, "How do you want to be remembered?" And I said, "Forget remembered. I just want to be read now." Everybody else had been talking about how they wanted to be remembered and which books they wanted to be remembered for. We don't have any control over that. It's not something that I worry about. I guess that's what I mean, too. You really *can't* decide, well, I'm going to write everything because something might be a wonderful hit. It's not something you can control.

Question from the audience (about what Octavia wrote in youth).

Butler: What I wrote when I was ten should have been put in the garbage. But, to tell the truth, I still have it all. The good thing is that it was written in #2 pencil on both sides of the page, so it's illegible now. It rubbed off on itself. But I didn't know how to write a novel when I was twelve years old, when I got the idea for *Patternmaster*. I didn't know how to write a novel when I was twenty. I didn't learn how to write a novel until I hit bottom, in a work-related way. It was, as I said, taking a lot of horrible jobs, and I took a job as a telemarketer. At that time it was called "telephone solicitation." I have a good phone voice. I am told I have a good phone presence, and I actually sold things to people. I'm very ashamed. But mostly I would call them, bother them, and they'd cuss me out. I'd call someone else. . . . This is why I don't cuss telephone marketers. I just quietly hang up on them.

I got laid off that job about two weeks before Christmas, back in the '70s. Any job that you get laid off two weeks before Christmas, this is a kind of disaster. I knew it wasn't going to be a very good Christmas. I actually cried about losing that job. If I was crying about losing a job that awful, it was definitely time to fish or cut bait. It was time for me either to write the novels, or get that civil service job that my mother had been urging on me, the one with the pension.

Still, though, I didn't know how to write a novel. NO idea. So I thought about what I had written. I realized that I did know how to write a short story. My short stories averaged about twenty pages long. I thought that twenty pages might be fairly decent for a novel chapter, and the way I wrote my first novels was in twenty-page increments. I was very lucky that my first novel, *Patternmaster,* was a kind of chase story, because chase stories have built-in endings. I didn't know at the time that I needed an end, before I began. If I didn't have an end, I wouldn't get anywhere. I'd just wander. I had been wandering, but when this version of *Patternmaster* became a chase story, this plan worked. I think of it as *a* method of novel writing, twenty pages at a time. That's how I managed to get my first stuff done. I did *Patternmaster,* mailed it out, did *Mind of My Mind,* mailed it out, got busy on the version of *Survivor* that was eventually published, and was about halfway through it before I had to go back to work.

Question from audience: How did you find research materials for *Wild Seed?*

Butler: I was very lucky. I had the Los Angeles Public Library, the main branch nearby. In some cases it would have one copy of something that looked like it had been mimeographed. I wasn't allowed to take it out of the room. So I had to use their copier, fifteen cents a page, and pretty much photo-copy the thing. There were others that I was allowed to check out, special loan. I was able to do all the research I had to do at the library, mainly because I had no money. I couldn't afford to go to Nigeria. I couldn't even afford to go to upstate New York.

I had just finished *Kindred,* and I was in a kind of depression. It was hard to write and not pleasant to research—that was the *real* research job, by the way—and *Kindred* wasn't selling. And I just drowned my sorrows in writing *Wild Seed.* It was *fun,* to my surprise. Shortly after that, somebody torched the Los Angeles Public Library and a lot of the stuff that I only got to see disappeared forever. So I was lucky, in that case. I had a lot of good stuff available. Why anybody would torch a library, I still don't know.

Hal Clement (from audience): People have been burning individual books for a long time.

Butler: I don't think they ever found out who did it. I blame the city council, myself. They knew that it was a firetrap, and for years they had done nothing. Remodeling was supposed to be finally about to start after years of, "Well, we can save money by not doing this, so let's not do it. We'll proclaim ourselves wonderful savers of the tax-payers' money. And then when it finally gets burned, Oh well . . ."

The way it burned, I'm not sure what to make of that. The fire began in religion and burned directly up to science, then over to social science, where there was a lot more water damage than fire damage. Somebody maybe thought this one out.

Q: This is what they mean by "intelligent design."

Butler: I hope not.

Question from audience: How do you go about plotting a novel which is essentially character-driven, as opposed to action-driven?

Butler: There's plenty of action in *Wild Seed,* but I know what you mean. I had to, because I wrote the end before the beginning. I wrote *Mind of My Mind,* and it was published, and writing *Wild Seed* was writing a prequel to *Mind of My Mind.* There was a real limit to what I could do. That was another kind of puzzle. I discovered, to my amazement, that I liked puzzles. I never thought I did, when I was in school. But I guess I like the puzzles that I choose or create. Okay, I have these two people and I know how they turn out. So, what can I do with them? That's what I had to figure out. It was writing in a box, and I really enjoyed solving the problem. How I did it? It's been a long time, but I find that I don't like to outline. Outlining to me kills the immediacy of the story. I guess what I mean by that is the more detailed outline. I have to know where I'm headed. I had to have that before I began the story. I had to tell myself the story in a sentence, although the sentence that describes that novel is not a good one. This just meant, "How do I get from here to there?" and what kind of divisions, time-periods, where do I want to head, and how far do I want to go with it. Sometimes history provides you with a kind of outline.

Question from audience: One thing I've always liked about the Patternist universe series, is that it is so obviously a complete universe, planned out.

Butler: I never really planned *Clay's Ark* when I began those books, but when I'd written *Patternmaster* and *Mind of My Mind,* I realized that I did want to know more about the Clay Arks, and I began asking myself questions. That's when I came up with the book *Clay's Ark.* I used to live in the desert of southern California, so I have been wanting to set a book out there for a long time. I think I got the idea for how to do it when I was on my way home from that Worldcon I mentioned. I had been in Phoenix, and I was taking a Greyhound bus home. I used to ride Greyhound busses all over the country. Ever so much fun.

And there was a storm. First it was a sand and dust storm, where you could barely see anything. Then it rained, and it was a mud storm, where you absolutely couldn't see anything. Sensible people were pulled over to the side of the road because they couldn't see. But Greyhound bus drivers have schedules. The bus kept on going. All I could think was, the driver didn't look suicidal, so probably he wanted to live. He must have been able to see something. I finally figured out that he could see the yellow line, which didn't really seem to be enough, but that storm is the beginning of *Clay's Ark* as well as an interesting facet in my life.

Q: Do you avoid outlining in detail because the books are a process of discovery, that you only discover what's in them by writing them?

Butler: Yeah. I do need to know, as I said, the end. Maybe it's a process of discovering how to get there.

Q: Do you ever get to the end and discover it wasn't the end you thought?

Butler: No, but I had a case where I discovered in the middle that I wasn't going to the end I thought I was. That was *Adulthood Rites,* which is the middle book of a trilogy. I thought it was going to be a downbeat book with a really bad, cliffhanger ending—bad in the sense that my characters would be in big trouble. But it came to a completely different sort of ending because my character insisting on finding a way to save some of what was left of humankind. Once I realized that was where he was headed, I just let him go and watched the story happen. It was fun to write.

Q: Thanks Octavia.

PHILIP JOSÉ FARMER

Q: You've written many stories, such as, most recently, *A Barn-stormer in Oz,* which revisit favorite fictional worlds. What is the appeal for you in this sort of thing?

Farmer: I think that basically what I'm doing is fulfilling childhood fantasies. I had always wanted to be a writer, and when I read the Tarzan books, the Oz books, the Sherlock Holmes books, and so on, I had the desire to continue the books beyond their range. I never got around to it when I was younger. In the past few years I finally fulfilled my childhood ambitions, but by that time I'd lived so long and read so much that they weren't really sequels. The books were expressions of my attitudes towards these series now, my desire, you might say, to make them even better but more realistic. I started with the Opar series, which I'm supposed to finish—it was originally going to be twelve books; then I cut it down to nine, then seven; now it's going to be five. And I might write one more Oz book. And of course, as you know, I've written about Tarzan and Doc Savage and Sherlock Holmes and a host of other people. I wouldn't call it therapy. It's just my childhood fantasies, and the desire to write something like an Oz book—which is quite different from anything Baum would have done, for instance. *A Barnstormer in Oz* is science fiction. I tried to explain a lot of the discrepancies in the Oz books, and, let's say, rationalize certain things that Baum didn't. He was writing fantasy and took it for granted. If you take the premise that the first Baum

Oz book is true, then you have to explain why these things are true, like the Tin Woodman, and the Scarecrow, and so forth, and how magic could work, etc. But then I also managed to combine another of my loves in this story, and that's early aviation. The hero comes through the green gate into Oz in a Jenny. Well, there's a lot of other combinations of things too. But I only go into the worlds of other people when I love their worlds, and I'm not doing any harm, and a lot of people are enjoying it.

Q: Don't you also consider yourself very lucky that you were born with enough writing ability that you can sell your childhood fantasies?

Farmer: Oh, yeah. That's a matter of course. It's something I never thought of. If I hadn't been a writer already, and had written those things to start off with, I never would have done it.

Q: What were the books that you remember reading that made an impression on you?

Farmer: *Treasure Island.* My parents gave me a copy of that when I was very young, and I read it several times. I think it had illustrations by N.C. Wyeth, if I remember correctly. Or Louis Reed. Jonathan Swift's *Gulliver's Travels* made a terrific impression on me, and the works of Mark Twain. Jack London. The Oz books. Edgar Rice Burroughs. A. Conan Doyle. Jules Verne. And one book that made a terrific impression was John Bunyan's *Pilgrim's Progress.* When I was a child I had a huge, illustrated volume of that. The illustrations were by Doré. I've been influenced by many branches of literature. Of course, what I loved most then was fantasy and science fiction. Most children when they read *Gulliver's Travels* see only the wonders in there, but Jonathan Swift's view of humanity also made a tremendous impression on me. That may be partially responsible for my semi-cynical viewpoint right now. On the other hand, *Pilgrim's Progress* made for an optimistic viewpoint, and of course that was a religious book. Then, I also read the various parts of the Bible that I could understand when I was very little.

Q: When did you discover science fiction as a recognizable field, as opposed to some books you liked which, in retrospect, were science fiction?

Farmer: That's easy. That was 1929, when the first issues of

Hugo Gernsback's *Air Wonder* and *Science Wonder* came out. I saw these books at the local drugstore, and Frank R. Paul's covers really grabbed me. Even though we didn't have much money then, I managed to get some money out of my father to buy those as they came out. That was my first contact with magazine science fiction. It was a golden day when I first saw those magazines.

Q: Did you get a sense of technological optimism from those magazines, at least for a time? That's what they radiated.

Farmer: Yes. Gernsback and a lot of his readers and writers thought that we could correct all our social and economic ills through technology. We could, too, if human beings were rational.

Q: Did you become disillusioned at some point?

Farmer: I was pretty much of an optimist regarding science and technology solving man's ills up until the time I wrote *The Lovers* in 1952. About that time I was having intimations that things were not going to go the way the Technocrats and Hugo Gernsback wanted them to go. Now, of course, I can see that whereas we have the *means* to solve our problems, due to economic and political and religious and nationalistic and individual human factors, we're just not going to do it. We're muddling along and we'll continue to muddle until something big happens. A lot of people are worried about nuclear war, and this is a justifiable worry, but I don't worry about that. It's either going to happen or it's not going to happen. What I do worry about, among other things, is our increasing loss of farmland, as against the ever-increasing population. The growth has slowed down, but the population is still increasing. You can draw two curves, which will meet twenty, perhaps thirty years in the future, when suddenly we're not gong to have enough farmland. I'm not talking just about the U.S., but the whole world. You can base a pretty grim prediction on that. It seems kind of ridiculous right now because of our present crop surpluses, but all you have to do is arithmetically base a projection, and unless something unforeseen happens, within the next thirty years there is going to be a general world-wide starvation.

Q: Gernsback definitely thought that science fiction had propaganda value and could influence the way the future turned out. Do you think science fiction has this ability?

Farmer: I think about the only influence that science fiction really had was in predicting space travel. It's possible that the German scientists may have been influenced by science fiction. I do think it gave the general population a sense of anticipation. I mean, if space travel had come upon us suddenly, without any preparation, it would have been greeted as a great, wonderful thing; but actually, with the science-fiction books and the so-called science-fiction movies, the public was ready for it. Now we do know that a number of people in the U.S. military fought against the idea of rockets, even when the Germans had demonstrated some of their potentialities with the V-2. It was only when the Russians put Sputnik up that the military had to break through their conservative shell and get going on that. But I do think that science fiction prepared the U.S. population for these space wonders. Actually, although there is a certain air of excitement about the whole thing, I think the general population is rather apathetic. The first man on the Moon was a big event, but people thought, "Yeah. They're going to the Moon. Sure. We've seen that in the movies." Actually some of the movies look more realistic than what you saw on TV.

Q: Allegedly a survey has been taken which shows that a large portion of the American populace doesn't believe the Moon landing actually happened. They think it was faked, because it was on TV and the effects weren't very good. But, aside from that, it seems we're living in the future depicted in 1930s science fiction, with Moon landings, atomic power, trans-Atlantic flight, television, and the like . . . only Frank R. Paul left some of the details out. Do you think science fiction can continue to be like this? Without the stories being overtly preachy "warnings," would it be possible to make the public aware of the diminishing food supply by simply writing enough stories about it until the concept becomes universally familiar?

Farmer: The trouble with writing so many stories about it is that readers become wary of such stories. They don't want to think of such things. I don't think that science-fiction stories about overpopulation have done anything to persuade the world to take birth control measures. What control measures have been taken have just come about naturally, mostly pioneered by people who were aware of what overpopulation can do. They weren't warned by science-fiction stories. It was their own thinking that did it. I really don't think that future science-fiction stories will have much effect on the general population, for the simple reason that they don't read science fiction. What they see in the movies, with a few exceptions, is not real science fiction. They're stories, adventures, and have no effect whatsoever.

Q: At what time did you know that you wanted to be a science-fiction writer?

Farmer: When I was anywhere from around twelve to thirteen, I knew I wanted to be a writer. I wasn't planning on being a science-fiction writer. I was really interested in doing mainstream. I just wandered into the field, even though I'd been an avid reader of science fiction in books and magazines since 1926. I still haven't given up on being a mainstream writer.

Q: Do you find it easier to sell science fiction and keep it in print? I notice that your mainstream novel, *Fire and the Night,* is not around anymore, while the novel version of *The Lovers* is. Is this a coincidence, or is it something about the field itself?

Farmer: I think if I'd had a very good agent when I wrote *Fire and the Night,* it would have come out in hardcovers; and if properly pushed, it could have become a best seller. As it was, it just fell by the wayside. However, I don't know that if it had been best seller, it would have been reprinted. One of the beautiful thing about being a science-fiction writer is that, although you may not make as much money as a mainstream writer hit it big—that was up until a few years ago, of course—science fiction is peculiar in that it reprints a lot of your stuff, and keeps reprinting it. I don't find that in any other field. over the long haul you can make pretty good money on it, and your stories kept in print. That was one benefit of science fiction I didn't think about. Actually, I had always loved science fiction, and I had some ideas, and I wrote "The Lovers" in 1952 and it created a lot of controversy and got me started. It may be that my unconscious was telling me that I should wait until I'd lived long enough and seen enough that I could really write mainstream. Now when I'm talking about mainstream, I'm talking about novels that have to do with today, with human characters. I don't know when I write this mainstream novel if I'll be using science-fiction techniques. Some of the people who have written science-fiction novels, like Kurt Vonnegut, but who deny it, are characterized by various academics as authors who write mainstream but use science-fiction techniques. It's all a lot of nonsense. Then others are characterized as people who write science fiction but use mainstream techniques. I've been working on this one main-stream novel off and on. I haven't written any text, but a lot of notes and so forth. Now Tom Robbins and Thomas Pynchon use what I would call science-fiction techniques in their mainstream literature. Perhaps it might be a fusion of the two. I don't know. What was the original question? [Laughs.]

Q: Whether it is inherent in the nature of science fiction that it stays in print longer than mainstream.

Farmer: It's a funny thing. H.G. Wells of course wrote his science romances, but he was very serious about writing propaganda novels, sociological mainly. Curiously, the stuff that the critics admired in his day, the non-science fiction, has not survived. Very few people read his other books. But the science fiction has survived. I'm trying to think of some other authors who perhaps wrote science fiction on the side, but only the science fiction has survived.

Q: Robert W. Chambers is a good example.

Farmer: Yeah, Chambers. The other day I was thinking about it, and I can't think of their names right now. But sometimes what the critics praise doesn't survive and what they deride does survive. The best stuff that H.G. Wells wrote was his science romances. And I've noticed that Edgar Rice Burroughs, for instance, who was not the world's greatest writer, although he did originate one of the world's great characters, Tarzan—his books are still being reprinted, while a lot of the books by others that were praised and were bestsellers in his time have dropped completely into oblivion. He's still here. There's something to be said for science fiction and fantasy having a staying power.

Q: In addition to it being a matter of no one reading the critics a hundred years later, it seems to me to be just one of the books that people want to read. The critics didn't like Sherlock Holmes, but he's still with us.

Farmer: That's it. It's what people want to read, not what the critics say they should read. Those are the books that survive.

Q: When you were writing "The Lovers" and other stories in the 1950s, this shook a lot of people up. Did you do this deliberately, from a feeling that the field was moribund and needed to expand its horizons, or were you surprised at the controversy?

Farmer: I had the feeling certainly that science fiction was a field that should treat all aspects of human life. A mature treatment of sex was certainly lacking in science fiction, and even immature treatments were rare. I felt that science fiction should be able to handle everything, like religion, politics, everything. I knew when I wrote it that I might have some trouble getting "The Lovers" published. In fact, as I have said numerous times before, Campbell and Gold turned it down with comments that the story nauseated them. I was very fortunate that Sam Mines and Jerry Bixby were editor and assistant editor respectively of *Startling*, and they were receptive. I think they saw the potentiality of it. They were ready to risk it, and it turned out not to be a risk. I think that most of the readers were ready For it. It was the *zeitgeist* that enabled them to accept it. If I'd sent it out in 1942, I don't think there would have been a magazine in the field that would have taken it.

Q: Were you left with the feeling that Mines was a better editor? I get the impression that in a lot of subtle ways, *Startling* was a better magazine than *Galaxy* or *Astounding* in that period. It was more innovative, and it also published the story that was too realistic for Edmond Hamilton to sell earlier, "What's It Like Out There?" He wrote it in the 1930s and couldn't sell it because it was, basically, too realistic.

Farmer: Sam Mines was not one for whom science fiction was his big, single passion, as with Campbell and Gold. He was interested in all types of literature. He'd written a couple of science-fiction stories, but had written many westerns. He wasn't worried as much about the reaction of his readers as Campbell and Gold were. So he thought: "Well, here's something that's really going to cause a sensation. We'll publish it and see what happens." It turned out all right. I think he was willing to take more chances than the other two were. Of course Campbell was willing to take a lot of chances on other things, but not in the realm of sex.

Q: Did you have any problems with the then-equivalent of the Moral Majority? Or was there no such element then?

Farmer: They were around, very strongly, but they didn't read science fiction then. There were some people who you might say really belonged to the Moral Majority, and I got a few letters from them. So did Sam. But there weren't too many in the field, actually. If it had been in a major national magazine—of course this would have never happened—like the *Post* or something like that, the uproar would have been terrific. But who cared what went on in science fiction then?

Q: You're commonly credited with opening this area up to a lot of others. Do you think you were the ground-breaker?

Farmer: I was a ground-breaker in that I did it. Ted Sturgeon of course had a lot of ideas too, some of which were turned down. When "The Lovers" was accepted, that did open the wedge for Ted to come in not only with new stories, but stories he'd written earlier. Still, there was a lot of resistance when I wrote "Mother" shortly after "The Lovers." Campbell and Gold didn't want it. By the time I wrote "Open To Me, My Sister," which later came out as "My Sister's Brother," Sam Mines had left, Popular Publications [The publishers of *Startling*] had folded, so I eventually sent the story to Bob Mills, who was editor of *The Magazine of Fantasy & Science Fiction*. He didn't want to take a chance on it. He rejected it. Then Leo Margulies bought it. He was going to publish it as the lead story in a magazine called *Satellite*. He had set it up in galleys, and in the meantime Bob Mills had been thinking about the story. He couldn't get it out of his mind. So when *Satellite* folded, he bought the story back from Margulies, and decided to publish it. I've got a number of stories that were bounced by editors, and they couldn't get them out of their minds, and decided to buy them later on. It's a phenomenon that doesn't happen too often.

Q: What was the result when the story appeared in *Fantasy & Science Fiction*?

Farmer: I really don't know, because the magazine didn't have a letter column. *Startling* and *Thrilling Wonder* had big letter columns, so you could get the reaction from the fans. This one? I don't know.

Q: Didn't the Riverworld series have its origins in this period?

Farmer: That's quite a story. I wrote the original Riverworld novel in 1952, for a contest. If I remember correctly, it was called the International Fantasy Award contest. This was a big deal in that a certain specialty press was going to produce the hardcover edition, and Pocket Books was going to produce the softcover edition. In those days there weren't too many science-fiction novels, especially in softcover. Pocket Books was putting up most of the money. I never got the $4000 check, which was a lot of money in those days. It turned out that the specialty hardcover publisher had diverted the money else-where, and Pocket Books was under the impression that the specialty publisher had the manuscript, and they couldn't understand why they couldn't get it out of him. Finally I got an agent and she found out what had happened. The hardcover publisher had me rewrite it once, telling me that Pocket Books wanted the rewrite, but they'd never actually seen the manu-script. So everything hit the fan and the specialty publisher went bankrupt, and I didn't get the money, and Pocket Books was so fed up with the whole deal that they didn't want to publish any science fiction for some time. Due to the fact that I had to rewrite the novel, or thought I had to, I wasn't able to write other stuff, and I'd gone into full-time writing as a result of my anticipation of getting money from the contest. It ruined my career for a number of years. I went back to work. Then a couple years later I started writing on the side again. But the novel sat around in manuscript form in the trunk for years, and finally I took it out and sent it to Ballantine. Betty Ballantine rejected it with the comment that it just seemed to be an adven-ture novel. I don't think she read it very closely. So I sent it to Fred Pohl, who was editing *Galaxy* by then, and he returned it with the comment that the concept was too vast even for a 150,000-word book. It should be a series. I looked at it and I agreed with him. So I took the original manuscript and used a certain number of the characters in it, but very few of the episodes. I changed the plot a good deal, but I still used the basic concept, and I wrote some novelets for Fred Pohl's *Worlds of Tomorrow* and *If*. Then I took these and put them together and expanded them, and produced the first novel, *To Your Scattered Bodies Go,* and the second one, *The Fabulous Riverboat.* Then some years later I wrote *The Dark Design,* and I continued that in *The Magic Labyrinth.* Right now I'm working on the fifth Riverworld novel, which will really be the final one. The reason I continued is that when I finished *The Magic Labyrinth,* I left myself with a tiny loophole in the last paragraph. I didn't know if I was going to take advantage of that or not. And then I got to thinking: well, here are eight people in this tower in the polar sea, who have more power available than any human being on Earth has ever had before. Can they resist that temptation? Can they use it well, or will they be corrupted?

Q: Even after all that, doesn't the original manuscript amount to an unpublished Riverworld novel?

Farmer: Yeah, it does, but unfortunately I only have parts of it. What happened was this: I had a carbon copy of it, but I gave the original to a convention. I can't remember which one it was. It was on the West Coast. Somebody on the East Coast purchased it. Recently I've gotten feelers from various special-edition publishers, who would like to print it, as a curiosa. But I don't know who bought it. I do have a carbon of the second version, the rewrite, and possibly they might bring that out. It would be quite a lot different from what came out in later years. I only used a small part of it, and four or five of the characters. In the interim between the time when I first wrote it and the time I started writing these novelets which were part of the series, the ideas in it had grown, of course, in a somewhat different direction. But Fred Pohl was right. I didn't really do the concept justice in a 150,000-word novel. It needed something more like a million.

Q: Could you briefly describe the content of the missing novel?

Farmer: *To Your Scattered Bodies Go* starts on the day when apparently all of humanity is resurrected along the banks of

the Riverworld. The original novel started twenty years afterwards. Burton was the main hero, and Mark Twain did show up
later on in the novel, but if I remember correctly, people like
Cyrano de Bergerac and Hermann Göring weren't in it. Joe
Miller was, and Lothair von Richthofen, the Baron's brother,
was in it, but that represents the list of people who were in the
first novel who appeared later. I changed the heroine from
somebody else to Alice Liddell Hargreaves. The mystery was
there, but the trip up the river was much faster. I changed the
ending too. The ending that you found in *The Magic Labyrinth*
was not quite what you found in the original. I did use a few
sections here and there, especially those relating to Joe Miller,
but otherwise it was entirely different in writing and in the
way the plot went. A number of ideas which are in *To Your Scattered Bodies Go* and the sequels were not in the original. If I
remember correctly, the original title was *Owe for the Flesh*,
and later I changed that title to *Owe for the River* for the second
version. "I owe for the flesh" is a quote from *Moby Dick*, where
Captain Ahab say that he is ". . . down in the whole world's
books, I owe for the flesh."

Q: Was the first novel designed to have sequels, or did it wrap
everything up at the end?

Farmer: I didn't think at all about a sequel. It seemed to
wrap everything up. But you have to realize that when I
decided to enter the contest, I had just a little over a month to
get the manuscript in. So I wrote the whole novel in a month;
and as fast as I wrote the rough draft and scribbled in rewrites,
Betty, my wife, retyped parts and a fellow next door retyped
—was Randall Garrett there then?—and Randall retyped.
Three or four different people typed the finished product as fast
as I was turning it out. I was working all day long, into the
evenings; and 150,000 words is a lot to get done in a month.
[Laughs.] It might not be for a old-time pulp writer, but that
was the first novel I had done. I didn't have time to think about
such things as sequels. I started from the beginning, which was
twenty years after the first resurrection, and went right on
through, and solved the mystery in the tower at the end. I
didn't think about a sequel. But you've got to remember that
the present Riverworld series is actually one long novel. What

I've done is start from the beginning, at the first resurrection, and work my way through. There's been a lot of wordage, but it's been a long river.

Q: This inevitably leads to the question of what your writing methods are like. Do you still turn it out with just one draft and some rewrites, or do you outline?

Farmer: I outline everything now, including short stories. An outline for a novel sometimes becomes two or three. I'll write an outline, and then I'll write another outline filling that one out and correcting it, and then sometimes a third one. I spend considerably more time on revision than I used to. No way now could I sit down and write 150,000 words in a month. But then I was young then.

Q: Do you follow the outlines closely, or are they just touching points for something that becomes spontaneous?

Farmer: You have to fill in the outline. That's the big thing. Quite often when I'm partially through an outline I will get an idea, and it will veer away from what I had originally outlined. Then you're on your own. But if you get something that's really radical—let's say you're half-way through the outline—then you sit down and outline from there. Very possibly you'll have to go back and redo the first part of the outline too. I take a great deal of time in working out the outline. But once you've done that, it's just a schematic or guide sitting over there as sort of a reminder, because the actual writing of the novel involves so many details you don't even think about when you're doing the outline. It's not exactly like the framework you put up for a house, because once you put up the framework, you know exactly what you're going to do. You have very detailed schematics. With an outline for a novel you have a framework, but you don't know then what kind of house it's going to turn out to be: Georgian, Cape Cod, or a skyscraper maybe. You might originally plan on a one-story bungalow and end up with the Empire State Building.

Q: What are you working on now? What's coming out soon?

Farmer: As I said, I'm working on a sequel to *The Magic Labyrinth.* And I have one more contract with Putnam's for a novel called *Dayworld,* which is based on the same society that was represented in my short story, "The Sliced-Cross-wise-Only-on-Tuesday World," where I had a unique idea for solving the overpopulation problem. I got to thinking about that. Of course the society is very sketchily done in the short story. The implications and the workings-out of that society were enormous, so I wrote two outlines for that. Once at a lecture at Illinois State University I even threw this idea out to the audience because I had certain problems. I told them and I said, "Now what do you think about this?" Some of them came up with answers and some of them came up with new problems that I had to consider. If my own perspective is too narrow, other people might see things that I didn't, which they did. This is the only case when I've ever asked other people to participate in the creation of a novel, but I thought they might be interested in the idea of solving the world's overpopulation. They were, and they were quite intrigued by it. So *Dayworld* is next, and then I want to write a mainstream novel called *Pearl-Diving in Old Peoria,* which takes place in the early '50s.

Q: Are there going to be sidestream Riverworld books, out of the main sequence?

Farmer: I had planned for two. I don't know whether it'll come out two or one. The reason I did that was because, due to the tempo of the novels, and also the wordage limits, I could not consider the many particular and minute details that would be involved in constructing vital societies, or into many, many problems that would arise. So I wanted to have a sidestream novel, in which I would not use any of the characters in the mainstream, but other people, and start right from the first day and show how this particular individual would be behaving and reacting in these societies which formed from chaos, and became in many ways completely different from anything that had ever been on Earth. There were a lot of other problems I wanted to tackle too. But the difficulty is that you can't write a sociological treatise. You have to have a certain amount of mystery and adventure in order to have a good storyline. You don't want to forget that.

Q: What do you anticipate doing after all these projects are completed?

Farmer: I have quite a few ideas for other novels, but at the same time I've started a number of series I should finish. I once sat down and figured out that I had fifteen series I'd started. Now a lot of people didn't know that some of these short stories are supposed to be the beginnings of series. I've got two more books in the World of Tiers series, and I hope to finish it up then. Three more in the Opar series. And once I wrote a novel called *The Stone God Awakens,* which was supposed to be a trilogy. I suppose I should finish that up. There are so many more it gets depressing thinking about it. I may not finish them all, but I would like to finish the ones that a lot of people have expressed interest in, like the World of Tiers. Many years ago I started a series about an interstellar Catholic priest, Father John Carmody. I left that poor guy hanging up in space with an egg growing on his chest for about twenty, twenty-five years. I'd like to finish that, because I've got about three more novelets in that series. I wrote a story about a super-intelligent German police dog, Ralph von Wau Wau. I'd like to finish those short stories. There's a lot of them. So much to do.

CHARLES L. HARNESS

Q: The one thing the critical literature always notes about your work is its relationship to that of A.E. van Vogt. Would you care to comment on this?

Harness: I was very impressed with van Vogt. If anything is good in my work, you can trace it back to him. He was my inspiration. I studied his plotting carefully, the way he interwove themes, and my work never came off quite as good as his did, but I tried.

Q: Did you deliberately copy his method, including the famous dictum of changing the idea every 800 words? Did you do this consciously?

Harness: I never did that consciously. I don't remember where I read it, but I did read at the time it came out [presumably in *Of Worlds Beyond,* ed. Lloyd Eshbach, Fantasy Press, 1947—D.S.] about how he changed his setting and approach every 800 words. That probably made for a good variety of narrative. I never deliberately tackled that, and I suspect that I in fact violated his rule many times.

Q: We do see that kind of narrative in *The Paradox Men,* where, every time you think you have it figured out, the whole setup of what the reader thinks is going on and what the character thinks is going on radically changes.

Harness: It could be. I wrote *The Paradox Men* in a kind of haphazard way, and I never really came to the point in my own mind as to what it was all about until it was finished. Then I had to go back and make everything conform to that idea. Of course the title has gone through several alterations that may reflect what I was thinking.

In the beginning, as I submitted it to a magazine, the title was *Toynbee 22*. It was to be the twenty-second civilization as predicted by Arnold Toynbee. Sam Merwin, who bought it for *Startling Stories,* didn't like that, and he changed it into *Flight Into Yesterday*. Then somebody, and I never figured out who, changed that into *The Paradox Men,* which of course is the greatest mystery of all. Who in Hell the Paradox Men are, God only knows. But it has been selling very nicely under that title.

Q: If you figure that out, then everyone else will know what is going on.

Harness: I had fun writing it. I wrote it in the spring and summer of 1948. I expanded it subsequently a little bit so it could come out in book form, but it seems to be well-read, and I don't really understand why. It is just very simple science fiction, using the standard themes, the standard denouements, the standard plotting. It seems to have done well, and I like it.

Q: I might suggest that it isn't standard any more than van Vogt is standard. As Damon Knight has suggested about van Vogt, the story's progression is almost like a dream on paper. It does not progress logically, but intuitively. You said yourself that you didn't know what the book was about until you had finished it. This suggests a book that is coming straight out of the subconscious.

Harness: I hadn't thought of that. There might be something to it. I used to write it on weekends. I had a full-time job at the time as a patent lawyer for American Cyanamid in Connecticut. I wrote, scribbled science fiction on weekends. I would try to plot something by Friday night to work on Saturday and Sunday. My poor family suffered of course—not too much, perhaps.

The book changed as I was writing it. It started out one thing and wound up another. The idea of circling back around the cosmos, I had discovered with my little daughter. I penned her up in a circular enclosure, and sat in there with her scribbling. She, like a little animal, went the circuit of the fence, around and around, trying to get out. So I thought, well, maybe I could apply that to this story and so I sent my heroes around the universe to come back before they took off. I worked that in. I had to go back, when I discovered I could do that, and change a lot of things, but everything worked out okay.

So, you see, it is very incompetently written. It isn't planned. It just turned out the way it did. It wrote itself, once I had the idea.

Q: I am sure there are writers who have to plan everything, so that they know that at 6PM next Tuesday they are going to be writing the second half of chapter 22, and they know what's going to happen in it, but I don't think most writers work that way. Have you become more deliberate with time and experience? Do you outline your books these days?

Harness: I don't know. Sometimes I plan it all the way through. Sometimes I just dream along and take what comes and hope that it all hangs together. I don't know which is better or worse. I'm not a really very skilled writer. In fact I can't recommend my method to anybody.

Q: You obviously have something. You have to consider how many other works were published at the same time, that no one reads anymore. I can't believe this is a fluke, because you've done it over and over again. I remember when "The Rose" was rediscovered and Michael Moorcock began beating the drums for you at *New Worlds*. Everything you wrote seems to have survived.

Harness: "The Rose" was written by pretty much the same haphazard method. In fact, I wrote a considerably longer version of it. I didn't like that, and I started changing it around, abbreviating it, cutting out. So it finally wound up to be what it is now. It was totally unplanned. The final product was not recognizable from anything in the beginning. It just turned out that way. In fact, right up to the end, I was making changes in it. I threw away the original, which is probably a good thing. But what as survived is a very neatly packaged little novella, which has some entertainment value.

Q: But you had some difficulty selling it, so that it originally appeared in *Authentic SF,* a very marginal magazine. But again we have thousands of other stories from the same period that are forgotten. . . . Did you get a lot of bewildered rejections from American editors? Why were you unable to publish "The Rose" in a major American magazine?

Harness: My agent at the time was Forrest Ackerman. He submitted it to every science-fiction magazine in the United States. Every one turned it down. For a long time I kept John W. Campbell's letter rejecting it. It troubled him, I think, because I brought music into it as a theme. He said that he understood "Pop Goes the Weasel" and he knew one other tune, but he couldn't remember what. He had to turn it down. So maybe the times have changed and it is acceptable now, but back then nobody wanted it.

Q: When you were rediscovered in the 1960's by the avant-garde—the *New Worlds* group—did you have any sense that they were reading into your work things that weren't there, or at least that you didn't know were there? You had a period of eclipse for about ten years, and suddenly you were rediscovered and proclaimed to be Art. What do you make of it?

Harness: I had stopped writing for a little while, several years, as a matter of fact. I had changed jobs and I was having difficulties learning a lot of new stuff and I moved from Connecticut to Maryland. I had changed employers. But before that the immediate reason that I had to quit was that I commuted to Lower Manhattan from Connecticut and this consumed a hell of a lot of time. It didn't leave any time left for writing science fiction. From there, I got back into it after I did move to Maryland, and I lived near the lab where I worked at that time. I got back into it, and I decided that I would write what I knew best, and this was "An Ornament to His Profession," as a starting effort. That sold very nicely. I've been at it ever since.

Q: Have you ever been a full-time writer, doing it for a living?
Harness: No.
Q: So it's somewhere between a hobby and a vocation.
Harness: I guess you could say that. When I was doing it, it was something between a hobby, a vocation, and a compulsion. And I loved to do it. Even when it didn't sell, I loved to do it. I wrote a lot of stuff that will never see the light of day.

Q: What brought you to writing science fiction in the first place?

Harness: I just wanted to see if I could do it. I wrote my first story for *Astounding* in 1947. I had read *Astounding* quite religiously for several years. I had just finished law school, and I had time, and I thought I would try it. John Campbell bought it: "Time Trap," one of the worst science-fiction stories imaginable. I think he was hard-pressed for any kind of story, and so he bought it. Now I can't remember what it was all about. I write these things, then I forget.

Q: If you go back and read your early work, do you find it to be the work of somebody you don't know anymore?

Harness: Yes, that has happened. Generally, it will gradually come to me. "Time Trap" is in my short-story collection, *An Ornament to His Profession*. I read that and I thought, "My goodness, this is kind of nice. But the next one—this is dumb." Then I'd read on. "But this is okay." I dragged "Time Trap" out, dragged it out. If I'd written it today I'd have shortened it. Then it was 10,000 words. It could have been said very nicely in six or seven, maybe five. So I don't know whether I'm getting better, or maybe the market is more demanding. I think it is probably more demanding now.

Q: Maybe you've become more self-critical. Any writer's condition is surely a mixture of self-criticism (too much of that and you can't write anything) and a release from inhibitions. So how do you release the inhibitions?

Harness: I've never had a writer's block. I never have any inhibitions. If I seem to have trouble getting started, I will start in the middle, then fill in before that and after that and gradually build it all up, and go over it, throw out this and that. I insist, Darrell, that I am not a model writer. I have no program to recommend, no system that can be reasonably followed with any kind of results. In fact it amazes me that I can produce anything.

Q: But you're still writing fluently now. So what are you working on now?

Harness: I took a year off. I have been spending time at the junior college with an Italian course. That had nothing to do with Science Fiction, but then I suddenly woke up in the middle of it here's a wonderful story about Galileo, in which I can work in some Italian. So I took some time off to write my Italian story, and I sent it out, and I don't know where it is now. There may be others with an Italian basis. I try to use everything that I get involved with. Originally I knew nothing but patent law. My stories dealt with patent law. But there are other things in life and I am looking into them.

Q: That *is* the secret. I heard someone ask Jack Williamson how he still does it and his comment was, "The brain still works."

Harness: Oh, he's right, and he's one of the grand old men too. I guess he's still going strong. I give him great honor. He's, what, 95? Remarkable. He's had a two-piece novel published very recently in . . . *Analog.* I started to call it *Astounding,* but you can't do that anymore. So it's a wild life.

Q: So there is something ideal about your career, as there is with Williamson's, which is that you've managed to keep adapting and changing. I am sure you can think of any number of writers who were at their peak at 1935 or !945 and their careers were effectively over ten years later, though they may have gone on writing for decades. I think of Stanton Coblentz or David H. Keller or Neil R. Jones. They stayed where they were. You kept moving.

Harness: I guess it's like winning the Nobel Prize in Literature. If you live long enough, you have a good shot at it.

Q: Did you know that Neil R. Jones was still writing into the 1980's? But he was still producing exactly what he was in the early '30s. But you're *not* writing now what you did in 1946.

Harness: No. It really changes with what I'm involved in at the time. For example, this Italian stuff with Galileo. A very neat little story of his trial which lasted four days. He almost got burned at the stake, but he had the good sense to say, "I give up." And yet it is reported that in a low voice he said, "And yet it does move." (The Earth around the sun.)

Q: So have your ideas of what a SF story should be changed over the years?

Harness: Darrell, I never had any idea what it should be in the first place. I read very little science fiction. Some of the *Year's Best* anthologies, some of the Nebula winners I look into. But that's all good stuff. I wish I could write as well as some of them. But my ideas change without any deliberate effort on my part, and it's all subconscious, and I am not aware of the change. So far as I'm concerned, I am still writing in about the same way in about the same style as I was sixty years ago.

Q: Do you ever go back to reread the older science fiction, what you might have read when you were young?

Harness: Once in a while I do. It comes in accidentally. I never go back deliberately. I never go back deliberately and read my own stuff. I publish it and I forget it, and I think that's best. The field is open for everybody, and let's forget the old stuff.

Q: You don't revere the classics then?

Harness: I don't know what a classic is. Give me an instance.

Q: *The War of the Worlds.*

Harness: Of course. I have read all of H.G. Wells, *The War of the Worlds, The Island of Dr. Moreau, The Time Machine.*

Q: And a hundred years later, we don't forget those.

Harness: Absolutely. Jules Verne is a little different. He's harder to find. He did everything very scientifically. *From Earth to the Moon* showed some of the problems that would be encountered.

The only thing I read, really, is books that people send me. If they look good, I look into them. And I can't read them all. There are just too many.

Q: I guess you intend to go on as long as possible.

Harness: I suppose so. It's hard to quit. I thank you for listening to me and letting me ramble pretty much at will.

(Recorded at Balticon, May 27, 2001)

MICHAEL KANDEL

Q: What did you begin your career with, fiction-writing or translation?

Kandel: I began as a translator. I don't remember the year. I started translating when I was a professor of Slavic languages and literatures. I didn't start writing until many years later, and when I started writing I stopped translating.

Q: You seem to have come into the field from a very different trajectory than most. Were you a science fiction fan, back when you were a professor?

Kandel: I was a science fiction fan in my youth. As I studied Slavic languages and literatures, I majored in Polish. I was reading a lot of Polish literature and I discovered there was a Polish writer who wrote science fiction. I really enjoyed this writer—that was Stanislaw Lem. I sent him a fan letter, and he responded and said "We could use a translator." He had just been acquired by, I think it was, McGraw-Hill. That's how I began translating some of his work. Then he moved from McGraw-Hill to Continuum and finally to Harcourt Brace.

Some years later I was looking for extra work and I asked Harcourt if I could get some freelance work as a copy editor and there happened to be a position open and I became an assistant editor at Harcourt. I started acting as a scout for another editor for some science fiction, and one day I got very excited about a book and the editor-in-chief said, "Well, why don't *you* acquire it?" So they empowered me at that point and I began editing science fiction.

As for my own writing, I had started a couple years before, and I didn't start going to conventions until my editor at Bantam said, "Now that you're an author you have to go to conventions and do what authors do." That's how I started becoming acquainted with the whole science fiction world. One of the first things I did was ask people like James Morrow and Gregory Feeley what I should be reading, because I had dropped out of science fiction for a couple of decades, and there was a lot of major stuff I hadn't read. Some of the gaps I've repaired since, but there is still a lot that I don't know.

I basically soured on science fiction in the '60s. I was still reading it from time to time, but I felt that it was getting too pretentious. So I stopped reading a lot of it.

Q: That's an interesting comment, because most of the writers who were alienated from science fiction in the '60s were usually the hard-science, *Analog* types, not people who would like Stanislaw Lem.

Kandel: I got involved with Kornbluth, for example, when I was trying to track down a story which had influenced a book I am working on now. I learned that it was by Kornbluth. Well, there were a lot of writers like Brown and Kuttner and Kornbluth that I really liked a lot, and there's a sort of '50s style. I enjoy that kind of quality pulp, and when a lot of science fiction started putting on literary airs, I felt that it often didn't result in good writing. Obviously there were some people who were wonderful, like Ballard, but a lot of the stuff wasn't providing me with the enjoyment that I got out of science fiction.

Q: At what point does something pass from high-class pulp into literature? I don't think you'd classify Stanislaw Lem as "quality pulp." But he's a science fiction writer, and so is Fredric Brown, and when you move from Brown to Lem, it's possible to turn the wrong way and get pretentious. So where does Lem cross over into Literature?

Kandel: These might not be the right categories. Maybe I just got tired of some things, myself, and turned away from science fiction, or maybe I felt that certain things were getting boring. Maybe there's a certain kind of writing that doesn't tell a story and gets a little ponderous and heavy and isn't very interesting.

Q: We're talking about the New Wave, aren't we?

Kandel: I guess so. Obviously there were some very good writers in the New Wave. I can't single out writers. I just have a general impression. I would pick up a book from the library and say, "Oh boy! Science fiction." Then I would start reading it and say, "But this is no fun." That was my response at the time.

I would make exceptions. I can remember reading Ursula Le Guin's *The Lathe of Heaven,* which is a favorite book of mine. But there was a lot of stuff which I didn't read, I wasn't interested in. Now I realize that I missed some really good books and I have to go back and read them.

I like many different kinds of writing, but what bothers me is writing which exists to show how talented the writer is, rather than telling a story or conveying an idea.

Q: Your first book, *Strange Invasion,* struck me as being like a lot of Robert Sheckley stories strung together. It's very much in the late '50s *Galaxy* mode.

Kandel: I guess that a lot of my heart is in exactly what you say. I was very pleased when there was a quote from Sheckley in praise of *Panda Ray* on the jacket. So, yes. You're right.

Q: Where would we place Stanislaw Lem in all this? He writes satirical, Sheckley-style SF too.

Kandel: Lem writes a couple of things which are a lot of fun. First, he writes straight science-fiction novels, like *Solaris* and *The Invincible,* which are, of course, worlds better in Polish than you have any concept of from the horrible English translations that exist. *Solaris* comes into English from French, and a lot of passages didn't make it into the English. *The Invincible* was translated from German. There's also *Fiasco.* Those are very traditional science fiction. The thought occurred to me that this was like H.G. Wells. It's gripping science fiction, it tells a great story, and it's thought-provoking.

Then I also love the humorous stuff, *The Cyberiad, Fables for Robots, The Star Diaries* of Ion Tichy. Those are a lot of fun, more in the tradition of Swift. Lem is also a brilliant writer of essays, which you also don't have much an idea of reading the few things that are available in English. So he's more than one writer.

Q: Lem doesn't really sell in this country. A lot of people find him ponderous. Is this just the reactionary American audience, or what is going on here?

Kandel: He's still in place. Harcourt Brace is keeping his backlist going. People are still buying it. They're not selling like hotcakes, that's true, but occasionally at a convention someone will come up to me and say, "I really loved *The Cyberiad*." I hear that all the time. That makes me feel really good. I see people take sections from *Fables for Robots* and put them on the net. People are reading it and enjoying it.

But you're right. He isn't wildly popular, even in Poland. When I was in Poland recently, people told me, "We find Lem kind of boring and heavy." It's true. Some of his stuff probably isn't going to last, but a book like *Solaris* will probably be around a hundred years from now. If it ever gets into a better translation in English, I think it will be part of the canon of science fiction. So he's not a perfect writer. He's written some books which aren't as good as others. But he is an interesting writer, the kind of writer that even when he makes a mistake it's worth going with him from page to page.

Q: Don't you wish you could get to re-translate *Solaris*?

Kandel: I have suggested to the publisher more than once that I would be willing, and I think it would be a good idea to do a decent, respectable translation of *Solaris*. But since there already is an edition in print, the feeling was they'd have a problem doing that. I think it's unfortunate. I've heard a lot of people at conventions over the years saying, "We would like to have a real *Solaris* translation."

Q: Is the old *Solaris* still in print?

Kandel: They're all in print in trade paperback from Harcourt.

Q: *Solaris* started off as a Walker book, and I think the paperback was Berkley.

Kandel: I could be wrong, but there is a big list of Lem available in Harvest.

Q: How much did you as a translator find yourself collaborating with the writer? I should think this would be particularly the case in the humor. I am reminded of something a German translator told me once. He said that when he was translating from English and he came upon a joke which would be incomprehensible in German, what he had to do was tell a German joke in its place. So people may well ask how much is you and how much is Lem.

Kandel: I think a lot of it's Lem. But there are some impossible to translate. For example, in a story where a machine writes poetry and someone says, "All right, see if you can write a poem where every word begins with the same letter." There's no way that you can translate that. You have to make up a similar joke, but in your own language. You have to do it in the spirit of the original, but it's your own. So there are places where the jokes are mine, trying to do something analogous to what Lem did.

There were some things I couldn't do. Occasionally a pun or a joke would suggest itself to me along the way and I would put it in later. I wasn't able to translate a joke on page 7, so maybe I could put in an extra one on page 12. Some of the stuff is mine, but I really tried not to do it unless it was really necessary. The principle is that it's got to be funny in English. Otherwise there is no point.

Q: I the translation of a serious, dramatic work done differently?

Kandel: Every kind of work has different problems. People would say, "It must be really hard to do all that funny stuff with all the word-play." Actually, I found Lem's philosophical prose much more difficult. This is rather hard to verbalize, but he writes in a old-fashioned, convoluted, ponderous style which is actually very graceful and has a lot of force and is very lyrical. It's hard to believe that, but when it works, it's really very impressive, even as it's difficult to read. Somehow, when you translate it word-for-word or idea-for-idea, it comes out oddly flat and sometimes pointless. That's probably more of an impossibility, if one impossibility can be more than another. Translation is a strange thing. You're basically trying to do something that can't be done and you're trying to fudge over it and give the impression that you've succeeded anyhow.

Q: Is the real *Solaris* sprightly and witty?

Kandel: The real *Solaris* is an extremely powerful and lyrical novel. There are descriptions of this sentient sea which are amazing. It's like prose poetry. You get the impression with these sentences that you're in the sea and among this amazing, unearthly seascape. That didn't come across at all in the English translation.

Q: What did you think of the movie?

Kandel: I liked the film. It's a Tarkovsky film. It's more that than it is Lem, although there is some Lem in it too, I think.

Q: Having come to science fiction from a different direction, from having been a translator and professor of languages first, do you find that this gives you a different sense of what you're doing when you write? Are you more aware of the language you use, as if you're translating yourself?

Kandel: I think it's a different mode. I once had the ambition to be a great writer, and I wrote a lot of stuff. I wrote poetry. I wrote novels. They were really terrible, basically dead on the page, and I came to the conclusion that I really wasn't a writer, that I didn't have it. In fact when Lem offered for me to be a translator, I said, "Really, a *writer* should translate you. I'm not a writer. I'll do my best if there's no one else."

After spending a few years writing a long novel that I eventually threw out, I sat down and did something that was silly—science fictional silly—and that was *Strange Invasion.* That had life in it. Somehow for me it worked to be non-scholarly and non-cerebral. When I was working at Harcourt, when I was copyediting work by Umberto Eco, for example, or Gunter Grass—which is pretty serious stuff; it has humor but it's literature—my writing was thumbing my nose at seriousness. I was having fun. So it was a different mode. I wasn't being a professor type or a literary type. As soon as I stopped thinking of what I was doing as literary, the writing seemed to have more life in it. That worked for me.

Q: What do we mean when we say it's "literature"?

Kandel: A good question. I don't have an answer for that. I guess I was taking myself too seriously, and when I stopped worrying about that and wrote science fiction, which I had always thought of as something that was not "literature" in the '50s, not mainstream, somehow the writing became more readable.

Q: Isn't it a somewhat schizophrenic stance to approach science fiction with the idea that it's good and worth doing, but not literature?

Kandel: It is. Sure. There is a lot which is not rational about writing anyway. Basically, writing makes me feel like I'm doing something worthwhile. I can't explain that rationally. I'm not making the world a better place by being a writer. I'm not improving anything. But I just have a sense of worth and I go with that. I really love to write. The writing itself is the most satisfying part of the experience. The other stuff, getting published, reading reviews, and so forth, doesn't come up to the happiness of doing the writing.

Q: I think that what we mean by "literature" is writing of genuine substance and lasting worth. But surely we can find some science fiction which *is?* There was "literature"

in science fiction in the '50s. You could cite *The Space Merchants* or *The Martian Chronicles* or whatever.

Kandel: Absolutely true. There's a lot of science fiction that is literature. No question. It is of lasting worth. But I'm talking about the stuff you read when you want a fix. You want to go to the library and have a great evening of reading something with blasters or dragons, or something like that. I was reading for entertainment, and I looked upon science fiction as entertainment.

Q: Is literature not entertaining?

Kandel: [Laughs.] Yes, you're right. It is. But on a higher plane. I try to write as good as I can, but I don't worry about writing for the ages.

Q: It seems to me that there are two ways to go wrong here. One is to very deliberately and pretentiously write for the ages. The other is to say, "Oh this is junk and I don't have to do it well." There must be a happy medium.

Kandel: I work very hard on what I'm doing and I try to write as good as I can, and when I read something I've written that doesn't work, I am capable of throwing it out, and I wish that some other writers had the ability to take something that doesn't work and chuck it, even though it's painful.

A couple years ago I wrote an experimental novel which was extremely clever and very boring, and after working on it for about nine months, I threw it out. I still feel bad about that because all that cleverness went to waste. But it didn't work.

Q: All your novels that I've read so far have been humorous novels. So I wonder if you couldn't have taken that experimental novel, turn it inside out and parody it, and make it work?

Kandel: It was darkly humorous to begin with. But my experiment was not to have an outline, not to know what was going to happen, but just to let one sentence suggest the next, just to wing it. There are some writers who do this, who don't know what's going to happen on the next page. That didn't work for me. What works for me is to have an outline. Of course as the writing progresses you change the outline as you get a better sense of what you're doing. So it's not like it's really all that well planned. But without an outline, there's no engine that's really driving it, and it's all cleverness. What I was doing was killing off the hero, the protagonist, and that was a symptom that there was something wrong. He'd come back to life again and be killed off again, but it wasn't interesting.

Q: Do you outline very closely? Your novels that I've read have all been rather episodic, and I would have guessed that you wrote them with some idea of where the ending was, but that you invented the rest as you went along. *Strange Invasion,* for instance, has a structure of a funny thing happens and then a funny thing happens and a funny thing happens.

Kandel: Yes, but *Captain Jack Zodiac* and *Panda Ray* were planned out. I think they have a structure. I don't consider them to be that episodic.

Q: Maybe people like it that way. You could have been the Douglas Adams of . . . whenever.

Kandel: I like Douglas Adams. Actually, I discovered Terry Pratchett recently. He was the main guest of honor at this convention I went to in Warsaw. I really liked him better than Douglas Adams. A very clever and very funny author. He writes these great one-liners. I don't think that's what I do. I'm not a one-liner type.

Q: Do you think you will continue to write humorous books?

Kandel: I will probably do what works for me. The novel I'm writing now is also something that is kind of dark comedy. The thing that maybe I'm doing differently and experimenting with is fiction that has more human emotion in it and maybe a bit more reality. I've done a lot of short stories recently. One of them sold to *Asimov's*. I didn't remember the story and I went back and read it and said, "This is really good. It has feeling in it." It's humorous, but it's got more sentiment in it. Hopefully that's true of *Panda Ray* as well. So maybe I am heading in a different direction in that sense, but I don't think I'm the kind of writer that would write something serious and straight in science fiction. Who knows?

Q: Have you done much short fiction before? Where has it appeared?

Kandel: Mostly in anthologies. There are about a dozen stories. There was one in *Horns of Elfland*. There's now one in *Omni Online*. It's called "Space Opera." Have you ever read a description of an opera written by a music critic? This is a description of a space opera. That's the joke and there's a lot of musical terminology.

Q: Have you read Brian Aldiss's novel *Space Opera*? It's a whole novel-as-opera or opera-as-novel, complete with lyrics.

Kandel: I was explaining to a Polish critic what the novel I'm working on now is about and he said, "Oh, that sounds like ____." He knows a lot more of science fiction than I do. A lot of people in Poland do. It really kind of amazes me. So I made a note of it. It is a problem writing in a field where you haven't read a lot of stuff.

Q: Of course if you give the same idea to a roomful of writers, you'll get totally different stories from each of them. This comes back to the general point that you came into this field quite differently. Most people started out as fifteen-year-old fans who want to write, collect rejection slips—

Kandel: I did that.

Q: But then you stopped for a while.

Kandel: When I was fifteen, I decided I would get a story published in a science fiction magazine, and I wrote stories and sent them to *Astounding* and *If* and *Fantasy & Science Fiction* and so forth, and I collected the rejection slips. The high point of the summer was that I got a letter from John W. Campbell Jr.—it was a rejection, but it was a personal letter—and he said, "I rather like your style. I suggest that you try us again." That was the closest I got at the age of fifteen.

Q: So your background isn't totally different, but still you didn't come up through the ranks reading every Ace Double, but from a background of world literature and translation and so on and discovering conventions relatively late.

Kandel: I heard the guest-of-honor interview today [at Readercon, 1997] with Kim Stanley Robinson, and he has sort of a similar story. He was an English literature student and he discovered science fiction rather late in the game. So there's a guy who is an academic and didn't grow up with it. I probably grew up with it more than he did, because I read it as a kid.

Q: Now that you're discovering the various traditions of science fiction as an adult, after your formal education is over, maybe you have more freedom to pick and choose what you want than would someone who had been immersed in it all their life.

Kandel: I guess there's truth to that. I am very opinionated, and I'm very picky. There's a lot of stuff I turn my nose up at. I sometimes think this is not a good quality in an editor because I do acquire books for Harcourt as a freelance editor. But that's the way I am. I'll say, "Oh this is boring" or "I don't feel like reading this," and this is true of mainstream as well. I have a hard time reading Henry James, for example, even though I know he is a great writer and I have read some of his work and admired it. But there is a lot of stuff I have a hard time reading. I suppose I have a mixed or contradictory attitude toward science fiction, liking the high quality pulp of the '50s and some authors along the way, and yet dismissing a lot of works.

Q: This may or may not be a shortcoming in an editor. One approach to editing is that you only acquire the sort of books which enable you to look someone straight in the face and say, "This is good." The other is the book you can't stand yourself but you know will sell a million copies. You may get the science-fictional equivalent of Barbara Cartland, and possibly the publisher wants that, or something that sells like Barbara Cartland. So, how do you balance the idealism versus the cynicism in editing?

Kandel: I don't really have to worry about the cynicism

because the operation I'm in gives no thought to a best-seller. I wouldn't know a best-seller if I saw one, and I have no idea what book is going to sell and what isn't. Having had some experience in publishing, I don't believe that any of the marketing or publicity people have any more of a notion than I do. They're all experts in retrospect, but they have no idea beforehand. It's always a surprise when a book takes off. I'm not talking about a writer who has an established name—because that is sort of money in the bank—but when *The Name of the Rose* took off, no one had any idea that was going to happen. No one. Of the few books I've done, there was one I thought was fun, a cute little book, but it would never sell. This was Jonathan Lethem's *Gun, With Occasional Music*. It did better than all the other books I did, as far as sales and reviews. I was totally surprised. But I didn't feel bad, because everyone in publishing is either disappointed by failure or surprised by success. So I'm not dealing with the kind of books that are known money-makers. They wouldn't want me for that kind of position.

Q: You must have an idealistic publisher.

Kandel: They're a literary outfit. They basically want books that have literary merit and potential. They would of course like sales, as much sales as they can get. They don't want to lose money. Of course. But I think they're very concerned about their image and reputation as a publisher of quality books, and that has been the message. Sometimes that's a problem because I'll like something that is just fun, and I'll get responses from the publisher that it's not on a high enough level. So it's a very different situation I'm in than most science fiction editors are in.

Q: Certainly most editors have to at least pretend they know how to spot books which will make money. Their minimum function is not to lose money for their publisher.

Kandel: I guess that's true. A very experienced editor, who is very respected in the community of editors, said to me, "Sometimes you hit a home run and sometimes you strike out, but your general performance is important. They'll tolerate a certain number of failures, but you have to do well enough times." So far the few books that I've done for Harcourt have done well, if not in sales of hardcovers, then in sales of subsidiary rights. So I have a fairly good record. And some of the writers who have left Harcourt and gone on, like Jonathan Lethem or Patricia Anthony, are doing rather well.

Q: Isn't it disappointing that you launch this person's career and then you lose them?

Kandel: Sure it is. But my first obligation is to the writer. Harcourt entered this period of downsizing, and writers and their agents were understandably nervous about that. If they felt there was an opportunity elsewhere, they went. There is nothing wrong with that. It is true that sometimes writers are too quick to think that the grass is greener in another house and sometimes that's wrong. And it is rather painful for an editor who discovers a writer and helps him. There is always a hope that there will be a long-term relationship. I think that's healthy for both sides. But practically speaking, an awful lot of people jump from place to place looking for better and wanting better for themselves.

Q: For the benefit of readers who haven't been following the publishing scene so closely, could you mention some of the notable books you've acquired?

Kandel: We did a few novels of Patricia Anthony, *Cold Allies, The Happy Policeman,* and *Brother Termite.* We did Jonathan Lethem's *Gun, With Occasional Music, Amnesia Moon,* and a book of stories, *Wall of the Sky, Wall of the Eye.* We did J.R. Dunn, *This Side of Judgment,* and now Jeff is an Avon author, and he's just had a book come out, *Days of Cain.* He told me recently that they're advertising it in *The New Yorker* of all places, which is pretty impressive. We did a book by Jean Mark Gawron, *Dream of Glass,* and we just had a first novel by a new author, Ian R. MacLeod, *The Great Wheel.* I think he's got a great future ahead of him. I am really confident that he's going to be a big name. He was in a sense a name before his first novel because his stories did awfully well. And there are other people. Kage Baker is coming down the road. I think she's going to make big splash.

Q: How do you balance the editing with your own writing?

Kandel: I'm doing both. I have a day job and I work often on the train. It's a long train ride each way, and I either edit or I do my own writing on the train. I get a lot done.

Q: So you have at least three occupations?

Kandel: It sounds that way. And recently I discovered a fantastic new writer. When I went to this Polish convention, they naturally gave me a lot of Polish books to read. This is the new generation. The first one I read, I had an inkling that this guy was going to be good, and he's so good that I'm probably going to want to start acting as a translator, which probably means I'm going to have to put my own stuff aside to do this. I'm not totally happy about that. The guy is such a dynamite writer. You've never heard of him. He's a professor at a university in Cracow.

Q: You might as well give the name so we read it here first.

Kandel: Marek Huberath. But it's a bit early to be talking about plans because I am still reading these stories. I haven't read since good stuff since, I don't know when. It's on the level of strength of a Bester or a Heinlein. It's absolutely wonderful writing.

Q: Is there a lively science fiction tradition in Poland right now?

Kandel: There are new writers. These are people who are a generation after Lem. Ask me this question in a few months after I've read these twenty books, and I can tell you who I think is good and who isn't. But I have a feeling that there are a few of them who are pretty good. But they're writing in Polish.

Q: Is their science fiction now the product of an independent tradition, or is it heavily influenced by American science fiction?

Kandel: I think it's a combination of both. They're influenced by the American, but they also have interests and styles that are Polish. They are strongly interested in social or political science fiction. That seems to suit their culture and their recent history in a lot of ways.

They also seem write darker stuff than we do. That's very interesting. There's a translation of a story that I recently edited, and I hope to be sending that to a couple of magazines here, by a young Polish writer, Tomasz Kolodziejczak. He likes to write about executioners—shades of Gene Wolfe—but it's different.

Q: Do you feel that you have an advantage as a writer being aware of whole traditions that most Americans have never read? Does this enrich your own writing?

Kandel: It's hard to say. John Crowley has said that writers tend to write from things that deal with their childhood. I guess that's probably true of me as well. The things that formed me as a writer probably have to do with my childhood, and it's hard to say to what extent I was influenced by things I read as a young adult, whether it was Polish literature or English or what-not.

Q: Thank you, Michael Kandel.

R.A. LAFFERTY

Q: What were you doing before you became a writer?

Lafferty: I worked for an electric wholesaler from the time I was out of high school, with time out for the Army, and after that for about 35 years. So it's mostly electrical jobbing. All sorts of electrical material I bought. About ten thousand items I kept stock on, and I got to like the business.

Q: What made you take up writing?

Lafferty: Well, it was just one of those days in the middle of life when I thought I might want to try something else, so I tried it. After a while it started to work.

Q: Didn't you mention somewhere that you were writing poetry before you were writing stories?

Lafferty: I was, but I didn't consider that commercial. Of course I have used a lot of those since then as chapter heads, and little verses I have scattered in. In fact I have used up all the good ones.

Q: How much of your past life comes out in works like *Archipelago,* which has an autobiographical feel to it?

Lafferty: Well, the background is authentic, in the war years and the cities and so forth. Possibly the five characters are composites of people I met along the way. In fact I was at an Army reunion with my old outfit just a month ago, and I recognized several of the guys in the book that I didn't know I had put in quite so definitely. I thought that I was writing fiction, but I found that there was more of the real people in several of chosen characters than I realized when I was writing it.

Q: Did you put yourself in it?

Lafferty: Oh, just fragments of me through all the thirty-five and a couple other characters there.

Q: When you started writing, why did you start in science fiction?

Lafferty: Well, I started writing everything. I wrote a *Saturday Evening Post* story and an *American Magazine* story and a *Collier's* story, and some sort of a western story, and science-fiction and mystery stories. I sent them around. The science-fiction story sold and the others didn't, so after several repetitions then, I just wrote science fiction. It took me about a year before I was selling.

Q: You have been quoted as saying that there are periods in science fiction in which all the stories are rotten, with exceptions, and periods in which all the stories are rotten and there are no exceptions, and that we are in a type 2 period at the moment. Why do you think this is so?

Lafferty: I was probably just in a type 2 day when I wrote that. Some days it seems pretty good, and some days it does seem rotten, but so does everything else. It was kind of a subjective judgment. Sometimes there are glimmers of hope for it.

Q: What do you see wrong most of the time?

Lafferty: Most of the time it's just gone down with most of the other fiction. It's not too interesting, and that's the cardinal sin of fiction, of course.

Q: You're somewhat unusual in being one of the few science fiction writers to use religious material. A few touch on it, and there are a lot of fake church stories like *Gather, Darkness!* but most writers seem to shy away from the actual substance. Why do you think this is?

Lafferty: Actually, religion is becoming more interesting, more important I believe. I think there's a lag. Most of them just haven't gone to that yet. There's the idea that religion is a drag, and so forth, but that idea is probably several decades out of date.

Q: It seems to me that science fiction often covers all the ground of religion, but does so in a non-religious manner. *Childhood's End,* for example.

Lafferty: Well, I think *Childhood's End* was religious, but that's more the case with fantasy than with science fiction. In fact almost all the high fantasy is really based on the Low Middle Ages of Europe, which is a very religious period. But all the religion is taken out of it, and the background of the Low Middle Ages, the Dark Ages, is used for sword and sorcery. They've taken the motive power out and used the furniture and costuming. I don't know why they did that. They're leaving out the main part.

Q: My experience is that often if a story even touches on such things, the editor will freeze up and think he's being preached at. You can write about, say, Hindu gods with no problem, but if you touch on Christianity, even if all the characters are doubters, the editor freezes. Have you ever found this to be so?

Lafferty: Yes, that's very much so. But you've got it backwards. The preachers are really those of a religion that is not called a religion, which is secular liberalism. That's really the established religion of our country, and of our world. It doesn't allow too much opposition. Now people who go down the secular liberal line don't want anything that challenges it. Hinduism doesn't challenge it because it is too distant. Christianity does, even Born-Again Christianity and the emotional ones. They have something that the secular liberal world is lacking.

Q: In *Archipelago* you talk about this sort of thing infiltrating real religion. What sort of response did you get from that book on this point?

Lafferty: Well, actually the only response to the book I ever got was from people I knew pretty well, who bought the book early. Now those people were already familiar with my thinking, and they went along with it, but lately I'm getting it from people I don't know, and some of it is kind of strong opposition. And I get some friendly pieces too. I don't know what the result is going to be there.

Q: You've stated that you think this is your best novel. Why do you consider it to be your best?

Lafferty: Well, I don't know. I just caught a lot of things in there. It's not science fiction, although the other parts of the trilogy are. It's really a valid piece of recent history, starting about 1943 and carrying on for ten years, and implying to carry on for quite a bit later than that, to the present. But it's really, I think, valid, almost modem history.

Q: It does have fantasy tie-ins, at least on a metaphorical level. You're dealing with great mythic archetypes who go out drinking a lot together.

Lafferty: That's a valid part of near-modern history. There's a lot more of those now than there used to be. [Laughs.] Boozy philosophy and so forth. That's become one of the new motive powers, of trying to talk things out anyhow. For better or worse it has.

Q: Have you ever seen any of those drinking stunts done, like the guy who broke the record before the contest, just to get in shape?

Lafferty: No, but I saw the contest itself. That happened.

Q: On a more serious level, what about the idea that science fiction is a form of mythology?

Lafferty: For that matter, science is a form of mythology. Myth isn't something false ordinarily. It's just a way of handling or coming on to a truth. When it can't be direct, there are lots of mythological things in science. They were in there quite a while before science was finally formulated. This is taking us quite far afield.

Q: Is this the reason for science fiction's popularity? It seems to me that if a literature works like mythology, it will push a lot of the reader's subconscious buttons, and it will appeal to him even if he doesn't know why.

Lafferty: Yes, but science is activated by a lot of those subconscious buttons. I was reading Newton himself on his optics last week. He was yawing all the way there. He believed in the corpuscular theory rather than the wave theory. He was actually writing mythology. Yet all his optic diagrams were valid, but his idea of how it worked, the corpuscular theory with little things bouncing around, instead of the wave theory, was wrong. Both are pretty much mythologies, really, because they can't be seen, can't be anything but implied. Radio waves—there's no way you can see them. You just get results from them. They were sort of myths for a long time, with laboratory people trying to find explanations for them. Corpuscular theory, with all these things knocking against each other, coming out with intricate results, is a myth. It'll give you the right answers, but is still wrong.

Q: Whenever you mention myths, the term "archetype" always comes up before too long. Jung's idea, as far as I understand it, was that these images or whatever are shared by all of us in the universal unconscious, and therefore anything which appeals to these will move us, because they're there, whether we understand it or not. Do you think this is the case in fiction involving myth elements?

Lafferty: In fiction, you're hitting it right there when the reader thinks he's the only one who had that thought and hasn't been able to say it. If you have a good one, every reader will have that idea: "That's what I was thinking and never could say." That is how the universal subconscious works. You may have dredged up something that hits everybody. Then you might miss completely. You might really be the only one who thought that; and leave everybody else blind.

Q: One is tempted to fake it, and make it up so persuasively they all think they did.

Lafferty: Of course you can never know whether they really did or they just think they did. If it rings a bell in there somewhere, there is some resonance that's on the subconscious level or some level.

Q: Speaking of making it all up, what is the relationship between your stories and the traditional tall tale?

Lafferty: I think I got the tall tales from my father, who was a great tall-tale teller. He first came to Oklahoma as a boy, and he homesteaded with these other young fellows. One of them was my mother's brother and one was her cousin, although she was still a girl up in Iowa. They'd each homestead a hundred and sixty acres, and they'd build a shack on the four corners together there. About all they had for entertainment was tall stories. That was repeated so many times on so many frontiers. You get the tall stories of the mountain men and the campers and the trackers and so forth. Well, there's just the basic American stories, and they keep getting handed down. I think I got mine from three master story-tellers I happened to be related to.

Q: How much of the traditional material turns up in your fiction, or do you simply borrow the method?

Lafferty: More method, because the tall story has to be spontaneous. You just start raveling one out and pretty soon things start to happen in it. Just like an exaggeration, it has to be spontaneous. The method is still there, the attitude to it.

Q: Do you write your short stories the way you would tell a tall tale?

Lafferty: I try to, yeah, but the handwriting gets in the way of it, if you want to put it that way. I think the oral tales are more authentic than the written ones that came later, and I think the oral ones are better. But you can't get them here anymore.

Q: Have you ever tried to tell the story into a tape recorder, then transcribe it?

Lafferty: No, I never tried that, but that's one idea. I told about an oral storyteller in one of my stories, "The Cliffs That Laughed." This was a Malayan. Now that's the only time I've touched that culture, but I guess there's a lot of them in the world yet. The Malays have a professional class of verbal storyteller. Now this particular one was a translator around the army base there. But he could tell them, and that was the way he made his living ordinarily.

Q: There are some Americans who do this on stage. I've encountered a little of it. Have you seen any of it?

Lafferty: Yes, but they're mostly anecdotes rather than stories, aren't they? I don't know. There seems to be a little difference there, or else I haven't heard the good ones. There's skits and there's anecdotes but I've never heard longer tall tales on stage, although there might well be now. Now that's not the same thing as reading, though, because reading gets a little bit artificial. The tall tale is being put together and told at the same time. It isn't just recited, or something already put together.

Q: Can you use any of this method when writing a longer work, like a novel?

Lafferty: I can try it, and I do it for short periods, but I can't sustain it, which is the main reason my novels are choppy, I guess. They're really just short stories strung together. I never learned the sustained novel very well, and what I do write in it isn't very good. So I was meant to write choppy novels or none at all.

Q: What are your writing methods like?

Lafferty: I'll do it several ways. I'll start a story going till it busts. Then I'll set it aside for maybe six months, and I'll write stuff that's come to my mind about that story in the meantime. Then I may start it at the first again, do some, and it may bust again, and I'll set it aside for another six months to a year. But I've done around two hundred stories and not more than a dozen have I ever gone through without busting for a while.

Q: Can you take the stories that have busted and never recovered and reuse their material?

Lafferty: Most of my best stories have been busted once or twice. Sometimes they're made out of fragments of several of them. They get the conflicts and contrasts in there that they weren't having when I first tried to write them.

Q: How do you tell when it's going right, when it hasn't busted?

Lafferty: When a story busts, I know it, because I get tired of it myself. I say, "This has gone wrong," and I stop before it goes further wrong. Sometimes I'll tear up the last two or three pages and set it aside, till I go back to where it started to go wrong. When the thing goes sour you can tell it. Especially when it's your own.

Q: Then you have to drop it, because there's nothing you can do?

Lafferty: Let time work on it, which may be the subconscious correcting it to make it back to what you meant to say there. With me it's usually about six months till that happens, though some are longer than that, and I try to forget them but they're still working there. Then I have better luck when I come back.

Q: Do you find that the writing of stories is a spontaneous thing you have to do, and if you don't do it for a while you get uneasy?

Lafferty: Sometimes the start is spontaneous. I get up very early in the morning and start writing like mad for an hour or two, but it's like I've got the thing started then, and I don't worry if it doesn't come the rest of the way. I'll either set it aside or go through slowly on it, or sometimes I'll work on two or three things at a time. I may write a day or two on something, and change to a different type of thing. But I really haven't ever written two stories quite the same way.

Q: Are you at all influenced by what is being published now in science fiction, either positively or by reacting against it?

Lafferty: No, I don't think I am too much. For a while I was, but it doesn't seem to influence me too much now. I don't know why. It seems like I'm more on my own than I ever was. I guess I get a little bit stubborn about writing my own stuff and not going along with those guys.

Q: Did any editor early in your career shape what you wrote?

Lafferty: No, unless Horace Gold did a little bit. But I actually had less trouble with him than anybody else did. A lot of those old *Galaxy* writers said he gave them fits. He made them change everything, and he'd seldom do that with mine. He did give me some pretty good advice on a couple of them and he was the first one who did. But none of them have changed me very much. The way I write seems to be too stubborn in me to make any real changes in it.

Q: To me this looks like a good thing. Otherwise everybody would write alike.

Lafferty: They say the style is the person, and if he doesn't write his own way, he has an awkward style, which might be, or he has a tedious style if he doesn't, but then if the style is the person there will be bad styles and good styles still coming out. There'll be bad writers and good writers.

Q: Given ideal circumstances, say, that someone has promised to buy the results and not interfere, have you got any projects you would really like to do?

Lafferty: No. I've got a couple things that I'm going to do, but they're not pressing. I'd like to write the last two novels of *The Flame Is Green* series, which I'm going to do someday. The first one is sold and the other two are not sold, so the other two aren't written yet. That's still one of the series I want to finish. There are quite a few things I'm going to finish up someday, but none of them seem real pressing right now.

Q: In a case like *The Flame Is Green,* where the first book is sold and the second isn't, what do you do in the third to make up for the fact that the reader hasn't seen the second? Or do you hope that this will generate interest and get the second published?

Lafferty: Well, that is a difficulty. I hope they'll be bought in series. Now this other series of mine, which consists of *The Devil is Dead, Archipelago,* and *More Than Melchisedech*—they're not really a series of novels. They're what I call simultaneous novels. Some of the years are duplicated, but from different viewpoints, and with different characters emphasized. This series was published backwards because *The Devil is Dead* was published ten years before *Archipelago.* But that doesn't make too much conflict. They're not really tied together closely, although the unsold novel, *More Than Melchisedech* does tie them together considerably.

Q: I have encountered people who claim they don't understand your work. What do you have to say to 'them?

Lafferty: I don't know. Maybe it doesn't matter if they do or not. I was talking to Barry Malzberg today. We both write a page in a little Italian science fiction magazine, and I told him that his column in that was the first thing of his I ever understood. [Laughs.] He said that I'm as obscure as he is and he's not going to change and I'm not going to change. Yeah, I'm a little bit confusing at times, but I say things as clearly as I can, but sometimes the things themselves are kind of intricate, and maybe it's better not to quite come off with something like that than to come off with easier things.

Q: Do you sometimes get editors insisting that you dilute complex material so the book will be more saleable?

Lafferty: No, the only editors I've ever had that interfered with me were Fred Pohl and Damon Knight, and that was mostly on short stories, although Damon Knight was the editor on *Reefs of Earth.* He was working at Berkeley then. No, I haven't had a whole lot of trouble but they don't influence me as much as I think they do. I could put it that way. Sometimes I'll make a few verbal changes and still not change anything.

Q: You mean make a couple of small changes and make them think you've changed something larger?

Lafferty: Yeah. You see, Damon always has this thing about ending. The ending of the story is the most important thing. Well, maybe it is, but I think that sometimes I wonder. The writer best known for endings was O. Henry, and I was reading through his stories just a little while ago as an experiment, and thinking, "Well, if he stopped that story just before the trick ending." And they're improved. You can come up with about three possible endings in your mind. Some of them are better than his. This cute ending can be overworked. Leave out a little bit there.

Q: In one of his collections there is a story that gets you by surprise in this context because *it doesn't have a trick ending*.

Lafferty: Ring Lardner did that years ago. A couple of them.

Q: It strikes me as a potentially interesting device. You start the story as if it is to be vast and complicated, and then—you get them.

Lafferty: I don't know if it makes much difference how you end it exactly. In *Archipelago* I ended it up in the air, of course, with everybody shooting at everybody. I'd rather stop right there.

Q: On the subject of endings, I think we're at the end of the tape. Thank you, Mr. Lafferty.

JACK MCDEVITT

Q: Let's start with the elementary stuff, what your background is, what you did before you started writing, and when you first discovered science fiction.

McDevitt: That goes back to 1940. I was introduced to science fiction by the old Flash Gordon serials, which I *loved*. My father seems to have had a passion for them too. The special effects, looked at today, are a bit strange, but when I was a kid, when I was four years old coming out of the Bell Theater in South Philadelphia with my father, those landscapes and those great rocketships were very compelling. I knew there were more stories out there than what I had just seen, and it got me looking for them. But that was the beginning.

I started reading Edgar Rice Burroughs when I was eight years old and became caught up with both Carson Napier and John Carter. I read the entire series. At one time I owned all the books. Later on, it was things like Jack Williamson's Legion novels, Hal Clement's *Needle,* Clarke, and Asimov that also reinforced my taste for science fiction. For a long time I was a very casual fan. I continued reading science fiction, I guess, until I started college. Then it was strictly occasional. I read now and then, some Clarke, some Bradbury.

Years later, when I became an English teacher and tried to win over recalcitrant kids who didn't want to read anything, I discovered Ray Bradbury. *The Martian Chronicles* seemed to me to be the most successful book in the world for getting resistant kids to start reading.

Q: Did you keep aware of what was going on in the SF field during this period? Were you aware of the New Wave, for instance?

McDevitt: No. I can't say that I kept track of it. I was a very occasional reader. For a couple of years I was a member of the Science Fiction Book Club and for a couple years I subscribed to *Galaxy*. I read some Clarke. I suppose I could say I was reading three, four science-fiction novels a year, but not much more than that. My reading went elsewhere, so much so that when I first started writing—I had been writing short fiction for two or three years—Terry Carr invited me to do an Ace Special. What was an Ace Special? I had no idea. That's how far out of it I was at the time. I was not keeping track of things. The New Wave rolled past and left me high and dry.

Q: So what *were* you reading?

McDevitt: Everything. I read mainstream fiction, a lot of history. I read books on science. I pretty much read whatever I could get my hands on, and, again, that included some science fiction, but I wouldn't describe myself as a science fiction fan during those years. I was a fan of whatever I liked. I have continued reading a lot of other things. Right now, for example, I'm in the middle of reading the Library of America volume of the work of Thomas Jefferson. And I'm on Volume 9 of Will and Ariel Durant's *Story of Civilization*. So I try to read other things as well. I read a ton of science fiction now, of course, because I vote for Nebulas.

Q: What suddenly sparked you to start writing it?

McDevitt: I was training customs inspectors at the Federal Law Enforcement Training Center in Brunswick in 1980. It was interesting, but it wasn't the kind of stuff that engaged your passions particularly. As a matter of fact I was getting a little bored with some of it. We were teaching people how to collect duty and where to look for the contraband, and that sort of thing, and I remember calling an old friend who had been the head of the English Department at Mount St. Charles Academy in Woonsocket, Rhode Island, when I was a teacher there, and I told him that I was just bored to death with what I was doing.

He said, "You know, you used to move ideas. Now you're moving freight." I went home and complained to my wife Maureen, and she said, "You've been threatening to write a science-fiction story for as long as I've known you. This would be a good time."

So I sat down and did a story about Ralph Waldo Emerson and the modern United States Post Office. I had always wanted to be a science fiction writer. I wrote my first actual science-fiction story when I was 19 and it won the Freshman Short Story contest at La Salle. They published it in the literary magazine, *Four Quarters*. That was the last thing I wrote, but it convinced me that I could write. Then somewhere in there I lost confidence. I took to reading Charles Dickens and other major novelists and thought, "There's no way I can compete with this guy," not realizing that I didn't have to compete with Dickens.

There were two things I wanted to do with my life. I wanted to write science fiction and I wanted to play for the Phillies. I did not make the Phillies, and I sat for twenty or twenty-five years without writing because I had no confidence in myself. So I wound up doing a story about Ralph Waldo Emerson. Emerson's particularly interesting because he's the guy who said you can do anything if you set your mind to it. If you believe in yourself, just go out and do it. So I wrote the story and called it "The Emerson Effect," and we sent it out a couple of times. It came back with the usual form letters. I said, "That's enough." I don't take rejection real well. I don't need to be hit over the head to understand the message. So I wanted to quit. Maureen persuaded me to sit down, take a look at the story, and bring in somebody cold who hadn't seen it before to see if there was a fixable problem. We brought in a friend of hers. The friend made a couple of suggestions. We put the suggestions in the story, and it went to *Amazing*. It came back from *Amazing* with a note that said, "We're full up, but it's a good story and otherwise we'd use it." I said, "That's enough. We're wasting our time." But Maureen sent it to *Twilight Zone* and T. E. D. Klein bought it. That was my first sale. I've always felt that if I hadn't sold the first story I'd never have written the second one.

But we've never looked back after that.

Q: Surely that was a pretty encouraging response from

Amazing. Did you know any writers at the time who could have told you that was pretty good?

McDevitt: Not really. Probably the first writer I ever met was Michael Cassutt. This was after my third story, "Cryptic," showed up on the final ballot for the Nebula. So we went out to the *Queen Mary* for the Nebula banquet in 1983, met Michael Cassutt, and discovered that, yes, you normally get form letters. You do not usually get responses from editors. But I had no clue.

I was wandering around, and suddenly I walked a bar and got introduced to Poul Anderson and Gregory Benford and it felt a little bit like having arrived in Valhalla. I kept waiting for somebody to come in and escort me out into the street, as if this was just not the place I should be. I don't know if it happens with everybody. I was forty-five when I sold that first story. You talk about sense of wonder. I have never quite gotten over the sense that I shouldn't really be here and be on a first name basis with these guys. It just makes the whole thing a great ride.

Q: Most people in this field start much younger. Maybe you can argue that you lost twenty years of writing by starting at forty-five, but in another sense you had an advantage. You were better educated and more mature when you started. Most people don't sell their first story and get a Nebula nomination for their third. Once you actually started, you shot ahead quite quickly.

McDevitt: I've been fairly fortunate. Things have gone well. My wife turned out to be a good in-house editor. As you know, Darrell, you've got to have somebody to look at this stuff and show you where the problems are and make suggestions, somebody who is not there to tell you what you want to hear but what you need to know. Yes, my career has gone quite well. I'm very pleased with it. Especially since I started writing full-time a few years ago, it seems as if things have really taken off for me. But I love what I do. You keep hearing that writing is this lonely business where you sit in a garret somewhere and don't talk to anybody for months. It turns out to be a pure joy.

Q: In science fiction, at least, there's this whole community of writers you get to meet and know. Did you find then, when you came out of isolation, that suddenly you were absorbing ideas from all directions? Did it influence your writing itself to suddenly be part of a community?

McDevitt: Oh, yes. The whole thing was an education, from other writers, from fans. I've discovered all kinds of things. I've mentioned to people before that what gets you in trouble with technological things, for example, is not the stuff you don't know but the stuff you know which turns out to be wrong. I discovered in the early 1980's when I was first getting started that I was just abysmally ignorant. I thought I knew basic astronomy and basic physics. But I was horrified to discover that expansion is not just expansion of matter, but of space and time as well.

Q: Meaning the expansion of the universe?

McDevitt: Right. I had no idea and I screwed up an early story on that, not realizing that while you might get a red-shift, you're not going to get a blue-shift, not for anything far out, no matter what you do.

Q: You became a hard-science writer, so you have to get these things right.

McDevitt: I've always had a lot of help. I guess I got a fairly decent reputation as a hard science fiction writer, but I don't really know a lot of science. I read pretty much every science book I can get hold of, and for a while I was a customs inspector in North Dakota, where not much happened and the nights were very long, so I was able to read a lot.

But the thing that really helps, I've discovered, is that you can call almost any expert in any field and if you ask a reasonably off-the-wall question, they love to get involved. I remember calling people at an observatory one time and explaining that I wanted to blow up a star. "What do I do to blow up a star?" "Oh, Jeez! I'll get back to you!" And they came back with an imaginative answer.

The first time I experienced that was for a question for *The Hercules Text.* "What might you see in a spectroscopic print-out that would tell you that the star is a construct, that it's an artificial star?" That was another situation where somebody said, "Give me ten minutes and I'll get back to you." And he got back to me and said, "Well it probably wouldn't have any lithium in it, because lithium is not important. A star doesn't need lithium to work. If you were building a star you wouldn't bother putting lithium in, but all natural stars have a lithium reading."

Q: I imagine that professional astronomers don't get called up by the likes of John Updike very much. They'd probably be more friendly to a science fiction writer, because you're writing about what to them is important; whereas somebody who is writing academic novels about infidelity might call up marriage counselors, but not scientists.

McDevitt: The questions had to do with things that are really mindstretching, the kinds of things that nobody ever asks in the field, but which are a bit challenging. "What do you see out there that would suggest there's an intelligence at work somewhere?" Those are things that, in my experience, astronomers love to think about and talk about, but in their careers they probably don't want to admit that.

Q: Also, a lot of scientists are science-fiction readers.

McDevitt: Not only astronomers or physicists. I've done a lot of work having to do with archaeology of one kind or another. Almost any kind of expert, if you're going to send him in a somewhat different channel, is more than happy to put himself out.

Q: Experts like to be experts, so when you ask one a question requiring expertise, *of course* he's going to go on about it. I also think it's the same impulse that makes people gather around in front of a news camera, to be in TV. It's a very basic human impulse. The expert would like to be able to pick up your book and say, "I helped him write that line."

McDevitt: I eventually went a step further. When I wrote *Ancient Shores,* I needed a team of well-known people to come in at the end and take a stand, but I did not want to use public figures without running it by them. It seemed to me a little tacky if I just drafted a dozen people and sent them in. So I had the opportunity to talk to people like Carl Sagan and Stephen Hawking and David Schramm at the University of Chicago. They were very good. "Yeah, plug me in. I'd be delighted to do this." There were a few who were perhaps not enthusiastic—not scientists, by the way. There were a couple people in academia who did not want to be part of a science fiction novel. But the scientists were all very cooperative.

Q: I assume it was an academic Literature teacher who didn't want to be part of mere science fiction.

McDevitt: Actually it was a couple of writers who were very reluctant.

Q: Academic writers?

McDevitt: No. Mainstream writers. One mainstream poet in particular. What I did was send out a letter that said, "Here's what I plan to do. If you're interested, let me know. If you're not, just throw the letter in the trashcan and you'll never hear from me again." And one of them turned the letter over to an agent who wrote me a letter threatening to sue me if I proceeded. It was ridiculous.

Q: What were you proposing to do?

McDevitt: Simply use her [the poet] as a character at the end of the novel, where I had a dozen people come in and say to the government, in effect, do not do what you're proposing. It's a mistake. That was it. It was very strange. But it was really the agent who was the problem, not the writer.

Q: On the basest level, we might speculate that the academic or mainstream poets, who have no readership, have a nice little gravy-train, and they don't want to share it with science-fiction writers, of whom they are probably jealous anyway, because science-fiction writers have a readership.

McDevitt: I suspect that's correct, Darrell. I tried to get Jimmy Carter, too, by the way, but I couldn't get through the wall of people around him, and they said, "Mr. Carter only publicizes his own books and not anybody else's." That was the best I could get.

Q: You must have picked up something from all these contacts with scientists. I noticed in your work when I first started to read it that you wrote very convincing descriptions of what it's like to be a scientist, what the daily lives are like, etc. I thought at first that you must have been a scientist.

McDevitt: No, I was an English major. Other people have said the same thing, though. I'm not sure that I have a partic-ular line on the lives of scientists other than that they're just as involved in their work as the rest of us are. They worry about mortgages and they worry about making a name for them-selves and being well thought of by their peers. I tried to treat them that way and I tried to go a step further and that is to make my scientists not generally the top guys in the field. I think all of us can identify with that. None of us is ever quite the top-dog.

Q: Anybody can read a book and learn science, but it's the experience of *doing* science that isn't written about very well, very often.

McDevitt: I appreciate the compliment. I've had the opportunity to talk with scientists and even to observe them periodically. I started when I first started working on *The Hercules Text*. I wish I could remember the name of the person. I called the public relations director at Goddard, told him I was going to write a book that was centered on the Spaceflight Center at Goddard and I would like to see the interior. They really threw open the doors. They took me around, gave me a chance to talk to everybody, took me back to talk to some more people. We went to a party in the evening. I could have spent as much time as I wanted down there. They gave me carte blanche. Other places have done the same kind of thing. It makes it easy. Scientists in the end are human beings. I ask myself, how would I react if I were working on a major discovery and somebody else publishes a week before I could go to press with it? It's just human beings in different situations.

Q: I'm thinking of a very human but most unscientific incident I heard of once, involving a frustrated archaeologist who was chipping something off an Egyptian monument because it was the wrong size to fit his theory . . .

McDevitt: Of course that's a violation of the game.

Q: Presumably your experiences with scientists was a self-replicating process, in that the more you did, the more you had to write about.

McDevitt: What I like to write about, I guess, is the questions that we really can't get answers to. I am fascinated by the size of the universe we live in, that business of the universe being so big a stage that it's hard to believe that humans are in any way central to it. You get involved in the scientific explanations for why stars develop and why elephants develop. Of course we still haven't figured out how life got started. But you keep running into these questions, like: why is there anything

at all? Why does anything exist? I know about quantum fluctu-
ations, but I am not sure that means anything to anyone, when
you really stop to think that a quantum fluctuation gives you a
universe. There's the issue of why the universe is so perfectly
adapted, when if you change the physical laws just a little bit,
you don't get stars. You don't get planets, or anything except
sludge. This raises the question of whether ours is the only
universe or whether it's one in a cosmic sea among billions of
universes. So I like to have people in stories who ask these
kinds of questions, and of course you can't answer them, so that
means you can play with them a great deal. But it just makes
for very powerful scenarios, and if you handle the storylines
and the characters at all well, you wind up with something that
works, like characters who have lost their faith, who have
looked too many times into the light-years, or have seen
perhaps that there are too many instances of, I suppose, God
getting lost in the concentration camps. Where is the interven-
tion? Why are we here? Is there an answer to it at all?

Q: For a lot of people, and not just the New Agers, these are
indeed questions without answers, so they decide not to *try,*
and to shut off the reasoning faculties entirely. Mystics of all
sorts do this. But there's a scientific method of examining the
universe, and arguably a science-fictional method, of applying
reason to these matters: speculation rather than faith.

McDevitt: The speculation is what makes the genre fun, to
ask the questions. To figure out which questions to ask. In
science fiction we can make up our own rules, and you can get
answers to the questions if you want to write a story that does
in fact give you an answer. But since we don't really know, I
find it more intriguing to picture somebody who is trying to get
to a conclusion and ultimately comes against that wall. There's
a story in *Standard Candles* that you commented on [in a
review in *Aboriginal SF*—DS] in which one asks the question of
whether there's a designer and what happens if you ask too
much. Is there a thunderbolt waiting up there if you get a little
too close to reality? But if there is a designer, why make men
when you might make angels? The business about, if there is a
deity, does he have a right to complain, since he hides himself
so well? They're just great things to play with, and since a

writer can stack the cards any way, you just go along with it. But since they're things we all like to think about, they make for good fiction.

Q: There are still some rules. You express a concern with describing the expansion of the universe correctly. The difference between science and mysticism may be that in science you can speculate, but you have to do it within the framework of the observable. So it isn't a total free-for-all, is it?

McDevitt: Oh, no. The science has to be right. But it's not really necessarily the science that you're looking at. Science fiction stories aren't so much about a given discovery as the implications of a discovery or a possibility. That's what's intriguing to go for. If we get involved with faster-than-light travel, we speculate on what happens to us if we really do get FTL. For example, I've always been fascinated by the that science-fiction people seem to assume that there are other lifeforms out there, that eventually there will be someone to talk to. There's a lack of evidence, of course, when it seems that after four billion years there ought to be some indication. Where is everybody? The Fermi paradox. Is anybody out there? The usual thing is to look at how it would affect us when we make contact. But another, for me, equally intriguing question, is how would it affect us when we reach the point where we decide that we are in fact alone?

Q: How would we ever know? There's always another galaxy to look into.

McDevitt: There's always another galaxy to look into, but if you've got faster-than-light travel, and you've been out there for, say, six hundred years, and you've looked in God knows how many places and have not found so much as a blade of grass, at some point, somebody is going to conclude that we're alone. That's not proof but we're not talking about proof. We're talking about when the society comes to a conclusion.

Q: You've just discovered the local neighborhood is vacant. You've just examined several thousand planets around stars in this arm of the galaxy and found absolutely nothing. That means this block is empty.

McDevitt: You may well be forced to conclude that what happened on Earth is some kind of special act. I don't know.

Statistics is a funny game. It may be that the mechanical events needed to produce the first living thing are so extremely unlikely that they only happened in one place. That's possible. If we draw the conclusion that that is the case, does that change the way we look at ourselves? I don't know. Would it, for example, ignite a period of decay, where we decide there is nothing out there, and if by then we have extended our lifespans, a lot of us leading virtual lives anyhow, do we turn the starships into hotels, relax, and float gently into the sunset as a species?

Q: Or do we decide, well, it's empty so we'll take it all over and shape it to our own will?

McDevitt: It could be. I don't know if the kind of society we're describing would go imperial, as Asimov's societies did, for example, or it's just not worth the trouble. Why are we not *driven* to go to Mars? We're not driven, I suspect, because the average taxpayer sees rock and not much else. How would the 20th century have been different if in fact we had discovered a few canals up there?

Q: I think it would be very different. It occurs to me too that the discovery of an empty universe would spark a religious revival, on the grounds that this is evidence of the Earth being a special case, and someone intervened.

Related to that, what did you think of the Martian microbes?

McDevitt: I was kind of surprised. Several days after the story hit the news, one of the television channels, I guess it was PBS, called in Jerry Falwell, and Stephen Jay Gould. There was an audience, obviously loaded with scientific types on one side and true believers on the other, arguing back and forth about the religious significance of the Martian microbes. I only saw the end of the show. But it's odd. I hadn't thought the incident had any religious significance. That should have been one of the first things that came to my mind, because it does send a lot of people over the edge. I was surprised at the degree of fury that surfaced on the show, people absolutely determined that there is no life on Mars, because it does create a problem with the Biblical story, although I am sure there will be an adjustment made if we find that they really are Martian microbes. My understanding is that it's still very much in doubt.

Q: Of course a Biblical literalist has a great deal of trouble with all the scientific progress of the last five hundred years or so. They have to deny absolutely everything about biology, physics, geology . . .

McDevitt: They can't even believe what we have learned about stellar distances because most of the stars are too far away for their light to have reached us.

Q: They can't believe in genetics. They can't work for the Center For Disease Control in Atlanta because they'd have to understand evolution to understand how diseases evolve out from under a vaccine.

McDevitt: And yet we saw statistics—my wife saw it; I don't know in what publication—that sixty-five to seventy percent of the population in my section of the country, which is the Southeast, still believe in Biblical creation and deny Darwin right off the top, or have never heard of him.

Q: Which means that science *is* an elitist occupation. Progress is created by the few. Most of the braincells of the human race have gone to waste.

McDevitt: Scott Adams—of *Dilbert*—makes the comment somewhere that once you realize you're living on a world with five and a half billion nitwits, everything begins to make sense.

Q: I've always felt that fiction, too, is an inherently elitist occupation. We can't aim for the broadest possible audience, because the broadest possible audience can barely read anything beyond a photo-novel. We might as well admit we're writing for the active braincells of the human race, not the rest of it.

McDevitt: It's interesting to take a look at the bestseller lists of today. We're apparently selling more books than ever before, but we have more people than ever before. If you look at the bestseller lists, they're all quick, easy, digestible things. Chicken-soup titles. John Updike was up there twenty-five or thirty years ago, but today we have all this kind of quick stuff that's very light and very easy to pick up. Yeah. We're changing. We're going downhill, apparently.

Q: I wonder if that's really true. Much of what was on the bestseller lists a hundred years ago was junk too.

McDevitt: I don't know. Sure it is. But I think there is a difference. I did look at precisely that a few years ago. Some fairly substantial novels were on the bestseller lists in the early '60s, as opposed to what's there now. But I'm reluctant to say we're going downhill, because that's what people always say, that we're in the last days of the empire, that we're on the way down. I don't really believe that, but I do think there are an awful lot of people who don't have a clue of what's happening in the world, and don't really much care. They operate in their own worlds. Maybe I'm among them. I don't know.

Q: Here's a science-fictional speculation for you. Let's suppose that in a couple of centuries the difference between the technologically literate and the masses becomes unbridgeable, so that the elite, that understands how things work has an overwhelming advantage in just about every area of endeavor. An obvious example is that if you don't believe in evolution, you can't understand how disease works, and you can't work in medicine beyond a very rudimentary level. Therefore the Creationists are *kept alive* by the Darwinists, literally. The ignorant masses are being kept alive, and fed, and entertained, and everything else, by a small elite of scientifically literate people. Presumably the time will come when it will become possible for the elite to alter themselves, in the sense of enhancing their brainpower, their life-expectancy. We may have a day in which there are near-immortal cyber-enhanced supermen running the world, but there are still medieval peasants out in the fields.

McDevitt: It sounds like "The Marching Morons." It's certainly not a world that John Galt would have approved of. You're right. We could well be headed in that direction. It almost does appear as if the division between people who read and people who don't is necessarily becoming wider, because knowledge is exploding all around us. If you don't bother to keep up with it, sure, you're back on the track somewhere.

Q: We may also find a world in which the great majority of the masses is unemployable.

McDevitt: We're always going to have to find a way to take care of everybody. We're always going to be caught with that situation in which those who are able to perform are going to have to perform for a lot of folks.

Q: Many of those folks are trying to stop them. What Jerry Falwell is trying to do is shut down the braincells of the human race, by turning everyone into Creationists, which would eliminate the scientifically literate.

McDevitt: I often wonder what Falwell really believes when the lights go out, but that's another story.

Q: Some have suggested that science fiction is a useful tool in this struggle to lead people toward reason and the scientific method.

McDevitt: We see scientists constantly telling us that they got their start from reading people like Jack Williamson.

Let me put it this way. I'm proud to be a science-fiction writer. I feel as if I were to die tomorrow I have done something reasonable with my life and have made a contribution, if only because somewhere down the line some kid might be inspired to do something constructive, or to have a career that is really enjoyable to him, simply because he read one of my books. I think that is a marvelous thing to be able to look at as a possibility. I think that the people who are writing can feel very good about that. It's a worthwhile thing to be doing. I can't imagine anything more worthwhile.

Q: That is, as long as you are writing your own original work that has your own original thought in it. I imagine if you were writing TV tie-ins, it would seem less exciting.

McDevitt: Yes. The obvious problem with novelizations is that you're limited in what you can do. You can't really develop the characters beyond what the requirements of the series impose on you. I wouldn't want to do that. I've had a couple of invitations to do novelizations. I avoided them. At the time they cost money, because my own books weren't going to sell as well as a novelization, but I think that for my career it was a prudent thing to do. It's worked out and I'm pleased with where I've gone.

Q: Thanks, Jack.

TIM POWERS

Q: Let's start at the beginning and start with when the writing bug bit you, and what happened next.

Powers: I had wanted to be a writer ever since I first read a book, which was *Timothy Turtle,* at about age 5 or so. I started reading all the kids' books, and I decided that was the neatest thing to be. I was, I think, eleven when my mom found me a copy of Heinlein's *Red Planet.* I was polarized, and soon found Lovecraft and everybody else. And then in '67, when I was fifteen, *F&SF* ran an editorial on how to submit stories. I immediately wrote what was just a retelling of a story in the same issue and sent that off to them. It got rejected, but I was real pleased with that because I had a *rejection slip.*

F&SF then, and maybe still now, used the backs of magazine covers for rejection slips—so I was just very pleased to have a real rejection slip.

Ever since then, I figured you might have to do some things like work in a pizza parlor to make rent, but writing would be the main thing.

Q: Were you told at the start, as many young writers are, that you can't write yet, but have to go out and experience life first?

Powers: Luckily I never heard that, probably because all the things I wanted to write about, you *couldn't* experience, the *Necronomicon,* galactic spaceships—you can't wait until you have experienced those things. What I have always heard and dismissed is that people would say things like, "Oh, there's a catch 22. You can't get published. Writers are all products of some specialist school somewhere, and if you're not a member of the crowd, you can't get published." That always sounded like a lie to me, and luckily it does turn out to be a lie.

Q: You seem to have progressed almost immediately to novels, or did you write more short stories first?

Powers: I wrote a lot of short stories, but there were several important parts of what a short story is that I was missing.

Plot. I could have interesting characters and interesting events, but it all added up to nothing. I got to twenty pages and had 'em all die, say. Then about 1975 K. W. Jeter sold a couple novels to Laser Books, Roger Elwood's old line, and Jeter said, "Quick! These people pay very little. It's brand new. They have idiotic length restrictions. There's no competition here. You get three chapters and an outline in right now and they'll have to buy it, because they have no other manuscripts."

So I scrambled and did that, and found that novel-length—of course what they were calling novel-length was like 60,000 words—was much more comfortable and much more likely to produce a plot than my 10,000-word short stories ever were. In effect, I never went back. I still find short stories very difficult.

Q: In a way you're very lucky. There's something you see in writing workshops—have you ever taught writing workshops?

Powers: Clarion, and Writers of the Future.

Q: What I've seen in writing workshops, which is the most depressing thing in the world, is this 500-page manuscript that is completely unpublishable and you can tell for certainty by page two. There's no grasp of the most basic storytelling techniques. Now if you learn to write by writing *novels,* don't you think you run the risk of being bad in 500 pages in exactly the same way you could be bad in ten pages?

Powers: That's true. Certainly Clarion students are always horrified to hear that an editor can *validly* reject a big manuscript on the basis of reading the first page. They always say, "But that isn't fair. What if it gets good on page 5?" You tell them, "Page 5 might as well be blank, man. Nobody's ever going to get to page 5."

I guess I just always tried to imitate real good people. I can see where I'm doing Heinlein and I can see where I'm doing

Leiber and a bit of Sabatini, and they were all pretty bouncy guys, getting the story moving right from the start.

Q: I myself took what I call the "coward's way," which is that you write short stories until you sell several before attempting a novel. This way you aren't going to have a whole closet full of unpublished manuscripts? Did you have one?

Powers: Short stories, yeah. I never attempted a novel until Jeter told me about Laser Books, and frankly, I don't think my Laser Books really were good enough to be published by somebody like Ace at the time. I think they really did need the artificial greenhouse of Laser Books. The publication of them was enough to get me totally committed. I quit my pizza parlor job and quit grad school and kind of burned the ships on the shore. But I *did* have quite a stack of what turned out to be unpublishable old short stories, which I think I pitched in the trash one day.

Q: It seems to me though that you've taken all the big risks—by plunging directly into novels, by quitting your day job right away—and gotten away with it.

Powers: I didn't even know what I was doing.

Q: The difference between writing a publishable book and writing for a living is a profound gap. Many people never reach the second stage.

Powers: Naiveté helps. I remember when I sold my two Laser Books and I got $1250 each. I wrote each of them in three months. I though, okay, this'll work. You do four a year, you make five grand. It sounded totally feasible to me. As it worked out, of course, no payments are on time, there's always delays, so I was actually living on more like *two* thousand a year. I can't imagine what I was eating. But luckily, after Laser Books went out of business, and after a bleak year where I had to go get my pizza job back again, I sold a book to Lester del Rey. He was a much more demanding editor and would tell you to rip the middle out of a book and fix up the beginning and the ending. At that point I was, in effect, getting real good teachers, people like del Rey.

Q: Did you have a feeling that it was an advantage to be bad in the relative privacy of Laser Books?

Powers: Yeah. In retrospect, I am. At the time I didn't know it was privacy. But, yeah, neither of the Laser Books was reviewed, except one in one fanzine. In effect I got to do the apprentice work in total obscurity. No one was paying attention at all. A whole bunch of people thought that my third book, *The Drawing of the Dark,* was my first book, and that was completely okay with me if they wanted to think that.

Q: Also you'd shifted from science fiction to fantasy at that point, and the real direction of your career was becoming apparent from your third book, not from your first two.

Powers: I think, really, fantasy was always the direction I was most comfortable with. In a way sub-divisions are always going to be arbitrary in the body of this stuff we all read and write, which includes Heinlein and Bradbury and Kuttner and Merritt and Bill Gibson and everything. But I think in my reading and also in what I have instinctively thought of as story plots, I have always inclined more to the Bradbury/Lovecraft end of the compass than the Heinlein/Hal Clement end. Heinlein/Hal Clement is too hard.

Q: But you do something quite hard, which is writing stories based on history and historical figures, starting with *The Drawing of the Dark.*

Powers: True, but there's an advantage to that. If you write things like Tolkien, Middle Earth, you have to make up the whole world, agriculture, architecture, economy, literature, etc. But if you're setting it in an actual place that existed, all those things are already laid out. You just have to go find them. If I set a story in Italy in 1820, I don't have to make up the architecture and economy. I can dig out what it actually was, and it'll be intrinsically consistent because it *did* function. And you get free, without having to make them up, such great color and drama and characters. In a way it's the easier way out.

Q: I think a lot of fantasy writers find the other way to be precisely the easier way out. Of course many of the wannabes feel that they don't have to get anything right because, hey, it's all fantasy anyway. When somebody says that, I usually reply, "You're doomed."

Powers: At Clarion sometimes I'll see this sort of wan fantasy setting, a default fantasy setting, and it's in a nondescript medieval world with lots of ale mugs in taverns and hardy aphorisms, and it's this weak-tea of Robert Howard and Tolkien, at tenth remove. There's never any question about, say, how could they have ships that go out of sight of land if you don't have good steel to make clock springs or if you don't have compasses at least? How can they have distilled liquor if they don't have any other evidence of the technology for it? How come the religions look like they would only be believed by morons? It's as if they *gesture* toward work that has previously been done by Tolkien and Leiber. But as a reader I am always not satisfied with that. I want the impression that the world exists beyond what's on stage. I want to think there are continents and weather conditions and earthquakes and stuff going on, which we'll never see— which of course the best writers do imply.

Q: As an editor I know exactly what you're talking about. Frequently the population of generic fantasyland seems to consist entirely of swordsmen, wizards, and tavern wenches. There's no middle class. No one produces anything.

Powers: You forgot one type, the princess who is a healer.

Q: You can get to the point where, when the story is based on a role-playing game, you can tell where the dice have been rolled.

Powers: [Laughs.] Yes.

Q: There's an arbitrary turn in the plot, that doesn't come out of character or anything that's been logically set up. That's where the dice were rolled.

Powers: Yeah, I run into a lot of people who tell me, "I'm about to start writing a novel. It's based on a role-playing game I do." I just want to tell them, I think you could get interesting characters or even interesting problems that way, but you're not going to get a plot. If the writer is aware of that, he can avoid some of the kinds of troubles you're talking about.

Q: I've always been afraid to get involved with role-playing games—

Powers: Yeah, me too.

Q: —because you use up your imagination and it's absolutely antithetical to real novel-writing.

Powers: I absolutely agree, and I think I would have a weakness for it. I have heard of some of these Lovecraft New

England role-playing games and Underground Armies. When I hear about these things, I think, God I bet that's fun. I bet that's a real kick. But then I think, Powers, there would go everything. Instead of getting damn little work done, you'd get zero work done. And, as you say, you'd use up all your cleverness in it, you know the little neat ideas that your brain coughs out every now and then would all be gobbled up by the game. And there wouldn't be any record of it.

Q: Do you go reading randomly through literature and history until something strikes you and then write a story about it?

Powers: Yeah. I don't know that the spur to an eventual book is research until it suddenly snags me. I'll be reading something for entertainment, just random, just flipping through a book until I see an interesting picture. Then I think, yeah, that's kinda cool. *Last Call,* for example, was started by reading a book by John Scarne on gambling. He mentioned that playing cards derived from tarot cards. I thought, well, that's interesting, because they're both spooky in their different ways. I might be able to do something with that. So, given that much, I went on and read stuff for a year, chasing it down. But, yes, it's always some totally unexpected spur. It might be something that somebody tells me. Somebody told me once that Edison's last breath had been caught in a test-tube and saved. I thought, well God damn, isn't that weird? Why would they do that. And that turned out to be a spur.

Q: One of the advantages you've gotten from this approach is that you haven't become typed as a generic fantasy writer.

Powers: That's true, right. If you keep a bunch of random books around to trip over . . . if you have random input, you're going to get random ignitions.

Q: So how did you get to be writing about spies in *Declare?*

Powers: I've always been a big John Le Carre fan. I do think *Tinker, Tailor, Soldier, Spy* is one of the ten great books of the Twentieth Century. For a long time it was my airplane book. Any time we were flying, I'd put that in my pocket, because I knew it was really long and really good. I finally had to retire it since I was beginning to know it by heart. But Le Carre wrote an introduction to a nonfiction book about Kim Philby, the

British counter-espionage chief who turned out to be a mole working for Moscow all his life. I didn't care about Philby, but I liked Le Carre, so I read the introduction, and Le Carre raised a bunch of intriguing questions in his introduction, which were not, in fact, answered by the text because, especially in the '60s, there was a whole bunch about Philby that just wasn't known. But I was thinking, well, Gee, you know, I could think of some answers to those questions. Of course they're going to be all about dead guys and ghosts and stuff, but you know, this might be an interesting basis for a book. . . . There I was committed for a couple of years at that point.

Q: The interesting thing is that you then put the dead guys and the ghosts in, where many writers would have written a straight spy novel. So what makes you create fantasy out of this kind of material?

Powers: It's weird. Since about 1975, I really don't read science fiction and fantasy a lot. I don't keep up. People talk about the hot new writers, and I might know them socially, but I probably have not read their stuff. Up until 1975, science fiction and fantasy was about all I read. So even though I mostly read mainstream type fiction now, my thought-tracks were all laid down then, and the cement hardened. I'm now just incapable of thinking of a plot that doesn't hinge on genies or vampires or ghosts or time-travel or something like that. Non-science fiction or fantasy plots just don't occur to me.

Q: Would you describe fantasy as a method for dealing with the material?

Powers: A method?

Q: You write about love and death like everybody else, but when you do it, the result is fantasy. Is this then a specific method for dealing with the world and with reality?

Powers: It's more of just a reflex, really. I don't ever pick it. It's just the only way I can think of to have a story occur. Therefore it does become a method, certainly. Inevitably if I've got a guy grieving over his dead wife, say, a mainstream book would go one way. He refuses to meet anyone else, or me meets somebody else, et cetera. With me it becomes, what does your dead wife have to say about your situation? I'll keep the problem of the guy with the dead wife, but the events are going to be given science fiction or fantasy developments.

Q: Do you find that when you write this kind of fantasy, you have to get the realistic details *more* accurate?

Powers: Yeah. I think all fiction needs to have as much tangible details as possible, to make the reader forget that they're sitting in their living room holding a stack of pages all glued together at one edge. But I think that fantasy, especially, needs to work to convince the reader that this is all tangibly happening, because if you give the reader a *moment* to remember that this is just a book, they're going to think, wait a minute, this is all bogus. Dead guys don't do this. There's no such thing as werewolves. This time-travel thing is impossible at its core. I think fantasy writers, way more than mainstream, have to keep running around and waving flashlights and stuff, just to keep the reader from noticing that it's completely impossible.

In fact, because of that, I think you even have to have your magic be plausible. I think readers are sophisticated enough to catch you on bits where, maybe inadvertently you've made it implausible. Like, I'd never have an invisible man who could see. His retinas would not be stopping light, if he was completely invisible. If I ever wrote about a three-inch-tall man, I'd have to think really, really hard about how much he weighs, how much brain he can have . . .

Q: How he stays warm.

Powers: How he stays warm. Very good. When you take his surface area versus his volume, the surface area is too big. And if I had levitation going on, I'd think, what are you doing in terms of General Relativity? I always anticipate that the readers are not illiterate about this stuff, and if I just blithely have some goofy violation of physics go on, the reader's going to say, "I may indulge you for a paragraph or two, Powers, but you'd better show me what really happened there."

Q: Then there's the other approach where the whole situation or image becomes a sufficiently outrageous metaphor that the issue doesn't come up, as in Lord Dunsany's *The Book of Wonder*. There's an edge of the world. You can drop off. Physics are not addressed, or relevant.

Powers: Okay, that's true. When you get into a certain kind of fantasy, fairy tales, let's say, there is a kind of pre-rational logic that applies. Chesterton talks about this, how in a fairy tale, if you pick one of those roses, a princess in a far-away land will die. There's some back corner of our brain that goes, "Oh, right, of course." If you can work to play to that part of the reader's brain, that is very good fantasy. I think of *Lud-in-the-Mist* by Hope Mirrilees, my favorite fantasy novel. I think among contemporaries, there's Kelly Link, a short-story writer. She can do that. Remember in *The Wind and the Willows* when Mole and Rat find Pan on the island? That takes a real mythic engine in your writing, which Dunsany certainly had. But I don't think I'm equal to it.

Q: I'm not sure it is even something you can do intentionally or deliberately.

Powers: Right. I think Kelly Link doesn't do it deliberately. I think that's just how she writes.

Q: There s something you can understand about it. The princess is beautiful. The rose is beautiful. They have something in common. It makes an intuitive, dramatic sense. Lots of would-be fantasy writers are doomed because they think that things just happen in fantasy without reason. The events in the story have to make dramatic or emotional sense.

Powers: Yes, that's right. And there is a kind of myth reason.

It's very hard to make a chart of how that might work, but books like Robert Graves' *The White Goddess,* which I don't think anybody could chart, gives you a feeling of almost being able to remember a beautiful, scary dream from when you were a kid. You think, right, right, I almost remember that! There is this kind of pre-articulate logic, which, as a reader I have a great time with, but as a writer, I don't think I can quite work from that level.

Q: Do you feel any inclination to go back to very early works which are written from that level, like Homer, or Irish myth, or whatever, and mine them?

Powers: Sometimes. I love Jung's idea of archetypes, that you can see some picture or situation and get this big resonance, which you can't rationally find an excuse for. You just think, what is it about this picture which has so profoundly affected me? I don't know. It's like . . . I've heard you can raise ten thousand generations of chickens in a roofed warehouse. They don't even have *legends* about the first generation of chickens anymore, and they've never seen the sky. But if you cut out a hawk out of cardboard, and run it on a string just under the ceiling, they all go crazy. They've of course never heard of a hawk. But there's this silhouette recognition thing in the back, back part of their brain.

We've got a lot of silhouette recognition things in the backs of our brains. And sometimes I have found a situation that strikes me as affecting in that way, and simply grafted it into a book. There was a section of T.S. Eliot's "The Journey of the Magi," about finding a temperate valley below the snow-line. There was the sound of a mill-wheel in the darkness. We found a room with vine-leaves over the lintel. It goes on and on, and you get the feeling that something is going on mythologically. God knows what, but especially that mill-wheel pounding in the darkness. Something's up here. So I just grafted that scene whole into *The Drawing of the Dark,* in hopes that it would affect the reader there the way it had affected me in the Eliot poem, and God knows whether it did or not, and God knows what the actual effect was, but, yeah, I just snipped it out and stitched it in.

Q: I remember how Sprague de Camp mentioned having read how the sultan of Turkey once put aside an island in the Aegean for retired executioners. It seems that when they went back to their villages, people wouldn't feed them, but they had served the regime loyally. Sprague imagined them sitting around in the sun telling old chopping-block stories. I think it's in *The Unbeheaded King,* where it would belong.

Powers: Yes, yes. That's a beautiful idea.

Q: I'll tell you one I found, and I did use. There's a story about the emperor Commodus, when he was a child, before he came to power. As you know, he was a really bad fellow. One day his bath-water was cold, and he went into a screaming rage, and because he was the son of the reigning emperor, the servants went running every which way in terror, and he demanded that the people responsible for letting the bathwater get cold be thrown into the furnace and burned to death. He would not be satisfied until some quick-thinking soul threw a sheepskin into the furnace, and so Commodus went over to the flue, smelled flesh burning, and was satisfied.

Powers: Wow . . .

Q: You didn't need any omen for that. This showed what kind of a man Commodus was going to be. I couldn't help but use that.

Powers: Yes. I think Commodus differed from other children in being able to indulge that, but I think the impulse to burn alive the person responsible for the cold bathwater is in every kid. I always think that *Lord of the Flies* is an inevitable picture of unrestrained childhood.

Q: I guess you're not a sentimentalist.

Powers: Not about kids. I get weepy about cats and dogs.

Q: From remarks you made about not wanting to stand between the reader and the story, I gather you don't have a lot of use for all this post-modern, decontructionist theory.

Powers: Well, no. [Laughs] The more I learn about it, the more deeply I hold it in contempt. It seems to me to be a deliberate, rational effort to unmake everything about fiction that they can get their pliers on. It strikes me as a parallel with what went on with painting during the Twentieth Century. Try to figure out what has been considered good about it, what has been effective, and then see if you can wreck that as carefully and as scientifically as possible. To me, fiction should have no purpose but to trick the reader into thinking this all is real. These are real people, and the events are happening around them. I don't care if it improves, educates, corrupts the reader—I don't care about that at all. All I want is that it be a totally convincing, vicarious experience that in fact is so good that you forget that it is vicarious. Anything that calls attention to its being fiction strikes me as pernicious.

Q: Bertold Brecht did this in theater, intentionally. He wanted you to go out of the theater without catharsis, discontented, so you would be a good comrade and support the revolution.

Powers: True, but Brecht, in spite of himself, had good characters. It's true that, say, *Mother Courage* or *Three-Penny*

Opera are kind of downers and deliberate disillusionments in their outcomes, but I think his characters are way more vivid and lively than he meant them to be. A playwright who, I think, does that perfectly would be Eugene Ionesco. He wrote a play called *Jack, or the Submission,* which is simply a deliberate attempt top get into the audience's mind and de-tune the fiction or storytelling-receptive circuits. I apologize to Ionesco's heirs, but it appears to be a calculated attempt to render drama impossible.

Q: I think it's done on the part of some critics because they cannot be creative themselves and they refuse to believe that anyone else can be either. It's like to Behaviorism applied to literature.

Powers: Yes, yes. I think critics did the same to painting in the Twentieth Century. I read and was totally convinced by Tom Wolfe's *The Painted Word.* This was what the whole abstract expressionist movement was about. While there are many very good critics, I think some critics take as their job to cerebralize and abstract whatever they see at the core of the form at the expense of whatever it was about the form that people actually liked. Paintings must not be *of* anything anymore. Books must not be about characters you could believe are real anymore.

Q: I wonder if this isn't a resurgence of the Protestant Work Ethic. They're afraid you might enjoy it, and that's wicked.

Powers: I like that, yeah. It goes with my idea that there needn't be any redeeming virtue in art, just so it works real well as the vicarious experience.

Q: I guess you'd say that in general a fiction writer doesn't have a lot of use for theory, and it might even be pernicious.

Powers: Right. I think that the only theories a fiction writer uses are more on the order of did you justify the presence of that character. Did the ending derive plausibly from what had happened before? Did you get the maximum possible effect out of that helicopter crash?

Q: The theory that I would venture is that the appeal of fiction is emotional first, and only intellectual at a very far-removed second level.

Powers: Yes. I think critics see that as being distracted by the trimmings and missing the core. They would say, "You're not supposed to worry about the Snopes family in Faulkner, in the sense of how they eat and does their roof leak. They're simply supposed to be representatives of something." I was on a panel recently where a woman said, "*Dracula* is actually about the plight of 19th century women." I said, "No, it's about a guy who lives forever by drinking blood. Don't take my word for it. Read the book. It is."

I think critics want to find the implicit message of a text, and they think that's the most important thing. I always think it's an interesting accident, and if some English Lit. major were to read all my books one day and prove there were never any themes in them at all, that wouldn't bother me a bit.

Q: Then it's the critics who have it backwards. They're the ones mistaking the trappings for the core.

Powers: Right. We disagree on what the core is.

Q: Well, let's change the subject and talk about what you're working on now. Upcoming books and the like.

Powers: The one I am working on now takes place largely in Death Valley and the area around there, which is sort of near where we live, say from Palm Springs on east. It's going to derive from complications which arose in the 1930s in Los Angeles, which are having consequences now. And if of course will be fantasy.

Q: Complete with dead guys and ghosts.

Powers: Exactly, yes.

Q: Thanks, Tim.

CHARLES SHEFFIELD

Q: I was impressed by a statement you made on a panel, that you went up to an agent and asked him to represent you, and when he asked what you'd written, you said you hadn't written anything yet, but were about to start. Things apparently went on successfully from there. Isn't this rather an unusual way to begin?

Sheffield: I didn't know it was unusual. I was about as ignorant as you can get. I had been reading science fiction since I don't know when. Like most science fiction readers and writers, I was a reader long enough ago that I cannot remember exactly when I began. But in terms of being a writer, I had no idea what you did. I thought the first thing, if you wished to be a writer, was to get an agent. It turns out I had it backwards. The first thing you're supposed to do if you want to be a writer is write. I learned that from Leslie Flood in England, and after he pointed out to me that writers normally had written something before they had an agent, I went away and wrote.

Q: You must have at least envisioned writing when you approached the agent.

Sheffield: I can tell you exactly what happened. I had been a reader of science fiction in my youth, and, as many readers do, I wandered away from the field. Then, in the 1970s I was traveling frequently to the Middle East, mainly to Iran, and I was trapped in London by a failure of a flight connection. Someone gave me a book to read. It was Larry Niven's *Ringworld.* I read it. I enjoyed it very much. And when I got back to the United States, I looked around for more books like it. I just assumed I had been missing what was happening in the field. Well it turned out that there were not very many books like *Ringworld,* and after I had looked around for a while and not liked much of what I saw, I decided that I could probably write books at least as bad as the ones I was reading. So that was when I went to Leslie Flood with the idea that I would probably be writing. But I hadn't actually written anything when I met him. He was very nice about it. Instead of roaring with laughter and throwing me out, he offered me great hospitality and pointed out lots of things about the writing business that I would have normally learned painfully and slowly. He gave me a few hours of his time to tell me what I should and shouldn't be doing.

Q: Did he ultimately become your agent?

Sheffield: He became my English agent. But since I was producing in the United States, he did that through my American agent. It was almost as if we knew he was going to be my English agent before I had an American agent.

Q: Did you sell the first things you wrote?

Sheffield: No, I didn't sell the first things I wrote. What I proved in my first attempts was that not only could I write as badly as most of the writers I had been reading, I could write a great deal worse. I have my first stories. Most people keep their first stories. I thought they were great, and I now think they are dreadful.

That seems to be a standard procedure, as writers keep on writing. The writer doesn't feel that he or she changes, but the stories change. It's almost as if something is going on that the writer doesn't know about, modifying the product. I now know why my first stories would never sell, but at the time I had no idea. I thought they were wonderful. That seems to be fairly common. One of the problems with material from new writers is that they've worked so hard on the story they think it must be terrific. That's the reason I don't like to do workshops. I don't like to tell people that things have fatal flaws. But if you want to help in a workshop environment, you have to do that.

Q: Then practice made you better?

Sheffield: Assuming that I became better. Writing, and reading what you've written, has some invisible, subconscious effect, but I have never been able to define it or understand quite what it is that makes a writer write better simply by writing and looking at what's written.

Q: Do you still hold the opinion that most of what was being written around 1970 wasn't any good, or were you merely out of sympathy with the kind of science fiction that was being written then.

Sheffield: This was, I suppose, the period in which the New Wave was having a strong influence on science fiction. As you know, the New Wave quite old literary technique, in terms of mainstream writing, being used for the first time in science fiction. The problem was that at the time these techniques were being absorbed, some writers became unnaturally obsessed by them, and forsook the traditional virtues of interesting plots in order to do stylistic experimentation. So the New Wave arrived, and was absorbed into science fiction, and eventually science fiction then took advantage of the New Wave but wasn't dominated by it. I encountered the New Wave before it had been digested, and I didn't like what I saw. I'm not the person to go to if you want to talk about experimental techniques in writing. I consider that I write very traditional, straight, simple, linear material, and if I make any stylistic experiment, it is an accident, perhaps an unfortunate one. Normally I don't go in that direction. My reading tastes are also toward strongly-plotted books with real ideas in them. The biggest thrill I get from reading is not the beautiful sentence, but the excitement of experiencing an *idea* in a story, an idea to which I've never been exposed before, and never thought of myself. That's where I get my kicks. That sets me apart from people who are looking for poetry in prose more than ideas.

Q: Do you think you caught a wave of your own? There was a reader hunger, about 1970, for more things like *Ringworld.* You've managed to fill that niche very neatly.

Sheffield: Larry Niven says that *he* benefitted from that backlash, but I was later. Remember that my first story was not published until 1977. I think by that time the New Wave had largely passed, but many of the books I was finding had been written at the beginning of the '70s, or even in the late '60s. Niven claims he was the principal beneficiary of a backlash to New Wave writing, because at the time he began, was around the middle '60s, he was at the time the only person writing hard SF of a particular type. I was a second generation beneficiary.

I was writing hard SF because I didn't know how to do anything else, and many people who had been admirers of the New Wave were still writing in that stylistic period. The problem with the New Wave was like anything else: once it's been absorbed, once it's been digested, it's a good addition. But while it's being digested, it's like most partially-digested things. It's not very nice to look at.

Q: So I take it that you don't take very seriously the argument that Samuel R. Delany has put forth, that there is no such thing as content. He has written essays on the premise that style defines content, that the way words are arranged on the page defines the reader's experience entirely.

Sheffield: That may be true of Delany. It is certainly not true of me. It's not true, I think, of most readers. Remember that Delany is reading and writing in a highly intellectual, analytical mode. Most readers do not read in a highly intellectual and analytical mode. They read because they want to have a good time in some way. They wish to be entertained. Delany is not a writer whom I aspire to emulate. Certainly he has great respect in the field, but he is not someone whose writings I enjoy. I would expect that Delany's comments, although they may apply very much to his own works, would not be the words he would apply to my works if he ever read them. I dread to think what words he might apply to my works if he read them. He and I, I suspect, are at the opposite ends of a spectrum in terms of what we hope to achieve in writing and what we look for in reading.

Q: Don't you think that it's generally true that any literary theory, when put forward by a fiction writer, describes that writer's work and little else?

Sheffield: Either that writer's work, or nothing, which is the other possibility. People make theories because we like to make theories. Theories have a certain beauty. Theories do not necessarily correspond to the external universe. In science, that which doesn't correspond to the external universe is normally rejected. I'm not sure that's true in the field of literary criticism.

I'm sure if you publish that remark it will produce reaction from others in the field.

Q: But others will enjoy it very much. But never mind that. What do you think are the unique virtues of the hard science fiction story, and why are so few people writing it?

Sheffield: That's two questions. Let me take the second one first. Why are so few people writing hard science fiction? Because most people feel they cannot. It's more a question of insecurity than of reality.

A hard science fiction story is nothing more than a story in which some element of science plays an important part. Anyone in the universe, or at least anyone among the people who aspire to write science fiction, can learn enough science to write a story based on it. That people choose not to do so, I think, comes from the feeling that *I wasn't trained in science. Therefore if I try to write hard science, I will commit some dreadful gaffe and everyone will laugh at me because I don't know any science.* That is, I think, a bogus argument. Science, if it's anything, is *learnable,* because there's nothing to it more than logic, facts, and theories. There is no subjective element. Anybody can learn it.

What do I think the place of hard science fiction is? The best hard science story is one that allows you to look at science, or the relation of science to people, in an interesting way. Sometimes the premise of the hard science-fiction story is totally implausible, and then the interest is in what it does to human beings. "Light of Other Days" by Bob Shaw is often pointed to as a very successful hard-SF story with many literary virtues; but it's not hard SF at all, because the basic premise, if examined, collapses. It's still a very good story.

At the other extreme you have, say, *Dragon's Egg,* Bob Forward's first book. Bob himself would say that the characters in that book, as he sees them now, are not very good. The real interest is that he's telling us about neutron stars. He's telling us about neutron stars in such a way that more people can understand it than would ever be able to read an article in a scientific journal. I regard science fiction a wonderful field in which science can be imported and made intelligible and made interesting to people who do not feel they can read the professional scientific magazines. Bob Forward is an explicit educator. He says that he writes primarily to educate. I write to entertain, but I happen to be fond of science. So I pull in science where I can, but I still want readers to enjoy the story as a story, not as a lesson in physics. The lessons in physics, though, were what I loved when I started to read. And I believed everything. I believed positronic brains were real. I believed in the swamps of Venus. Only later did I learn that you have to separate the invented science from the real science. I try in my own stories, whenever I'm allowed to, to write some sort of explanatory appendix that says, "Look, I invented these things, but all these other things are science as we know it today." Usually editors don't want me to do that, but I like to do it.

Q: Couldn't the purely educational aspect that Bob Forward is talking about have been handled just as well in non-fiction, in an Isaac Asimov article?

Sheffield: Or an Isaac Asimov story. Many of Asimov's stories actually have a tutorial function. No one ever criticized Asimov for the lack of clarity of expression of his ideas. That was one of his great virtues. His articles had clarity, and his stories had clarity. But there are many people who will pick up and read an Asimov story, who would not think of picking up and reading an Asimov article on a scientific subject. They say, "I'm not interested in science, but I do like fiction, and Isaac Asimov is one of my favorite writers."

When you write a science article, the single most important thing is clarity. If you have to use the same word repeatedly in successive sentences to optimize the clarity of what you're getting across, you do it. In fiction, what you leave out is as important as what you put in, and clarity is not your primary intent.

Of course, when you write hard SF, you're also trying to write acceptable fiction. The tricky piece is avoiding expository lumps. It's easy to write a story in which you stop the action and have one character explain to the other character things that they both already know, in order to tell it to the reader. I don't teach writing, but I suspect that courses in writing say "Don't do this" very early on. The trick in hard SF is to get the ideas across clearly, but make them invisible, so the reader does not feel there is an education process going on. At the same time, you only put enough of the idea in to be clear, and you don't beat it to death. I'll quote Voltaire, but in English: *To say everything is to bore.* I think that's true in fiction. But it's a fine line. If you try to tell the reader everything on a subject, that's almost always too much. If you put in too little, and it's about science, the reader won't know what you're talking about. There are two reasons why writers do that. One is a failure of storytelling technique, in which you don't realize you haven't put enough in. The other is that the writer doesn't know the subject.

If you don't know enough about a topic, you may write at the limit of your own knowledge. I have a rule, that if I'm going to write about a scientific idea, I have to know ten times as much as I write. I don't want to feel that I'm at the boundary of my own knowledge, because I suspect that comes across to a reader.

Q: To get back to something you said a little earlier, I think that there are two reasons some writers shy away from hard science fiction. One is an inability to extrapolate science imaginatively, rather than just take standard ideas off somebody else's shelf. The other is an inability to depict what it is like to *do* science. I think that what a hard science story often requires is the ability to depict the day-to-day lives and personalities and habits of people who work in laboratories and actually make scientific discoveries. It's the *experience* of science which we get from the hard science story, as well as the actual content of science.

Sheffield: It's not true just of hard science. One of the reasons there are so many books and stories involving writers is because that's what writers know. You might say that someone who writes a story set on a submarine has exactly the same problem. They don't know what it's like, normally, to have been on a submarine underwater for two months, and therefore they can't write plausibly and realistically about that life. I think that is a constraint on people writing hard-SF stories, but it really shouldn't be because most readers have not spent two months on a submarine either. I write quite comfortably and probably ignorantly about biology and medical science. In those areas, I have no training whatsoever. But I don't mind. I feel that I have as much as I need to know in order for my reader to feel comfortable. If I'm wrong, they'll write me outraged letters or respond in some other way. But you may be right that the feeling of doing science is important if you're writing a story in which scientists are interacting with scientists. If you write a story in which scientists are interacting with people who are not scientists, you don't really have that problem, because then the other players in the story will require the same explanations that the reader will require. They will demand it of the scientist, who then has an opportunity to put in layman's terms what the science is.

I still think the main reason people don't do it is a lack of confidence. I'm just finishing a book called *The Borderlands of Science and Science Fiction,* and what I set out to do is to say, look, here are the boundaries of science, in terms of biology, chemistry, physics, and so on, and here are what I call the offshore areas, in which anything you write will be science fiction. The professional scientist will say "That's beyond what we know," but won't say it's so far beyond what we know that it's outright fantasy. I'm spending a whole book defining these coastal zones. I hope that one of the things this will do is encourage people to write offshore from the scientific mainland.

It's partially simple knowledge, but more than that it is lack of confidence that limits what we write about. One reason I write about biology and chemistry, I suppose, is that I don't really care that people will think I'm an idiot. If I do something egregiously wrong in biology, that's bad, but it's not as bad as if I do something wrong in physics. I'm supposed to *know* physics. I feel that if you don't know science, you have a much greater freedom to write about science than if you do, because you're completely unshackled. You aren't bound to any body of discipline that you must observe; whereas I cannot easily violate certain physical laws in what I write.

If I don't accept the limitation of the speed of light, then I have to find a way around it; most people can just say, "Well we had this FTL drive, and off we went."

Q: Isn't talking your way around it the whole issue? If you actually *knew* how to get around the limit of the speed of light, you'd be collecting your Nobel Prize. But the issue is one of reader confidence. You don't want the reader to say, "This doesn't make sense. This guy doesn't know what he's talking about." The trick is to reassure the reader that you've thought of that, even if we all agree your actual explanation is nonsense. Isn't that the essence of faking it?

Sheffield: It is. The faster-than-light drive is perhaps not the best example, because most readers take that as one of the trappings of the field. You don't have to explain it. But if you take something else, something which is against the accepted scientific wisdom, and it's not already used in science fiction, then you have to do some explanation.

For instance, I would probably have to explain magnetic monopoles if I used them in a story. They've been used many times, but I would still feel obligated to say something about the fact that we have either manufactured them or discovered them. An FTL drive, I don't have to explain. If I just say "We were on a journey from one of the galactic arms to another," the science-fiction reader knows there is an FTL drive, because the reader knows we're talking about thousands of light-years. The trip is not presumed to take many millions of years. Therefore, in the background, in the reader's head, is a faster-than-light drive. It's only when you're putting something in that is not a staple, standby element of science fiction that you feel obliged to explain. For example, you can't just write a story—or I suppose I mean I couldn't—in which everybody lives five thousand years. I would feel obliged to put in an explanation as to what happened. How did we get from a mean life expectancy of between seventy and a hundred to a mean life expectancy of five thousand? In my stories, that would almost certainly be a big element. It wouldn't just be, "Back in the year 2010, they discovered this drug which enabled us to live for five thousand years." I would feel cheated by that statement. I want to know what happened. I want to know how it happened, and what it did to society when suddenly everyone lived so long, and so on. But faster-than-light drives, I don't have to explain. I can introduce it as a background element and go on with the story without thinking twice about it.

Q: Don't you also need, to write hard science fiction, some confidence in the believability of your story, in order to give it emotional conviction?

Sheffield: It depends on the individual. If I think there's something wrong with the science underpinnings of the story, I would feel very uncomfortable writing it. That would probably show up, too, unless I am better at faking it than I used to be. It may be a matter of experience.

I've heard it said on a panel that there's nothing for which you cannot create a satisfying story, regardless of explanation. You pick something—teleportation, telepathy, faster-than-light travel. And you just use it. For instance, *The Stars My Destination* has teleportation. We don't worry about that. It's a wonderful story. We accept it. *The Demolished Man,* to cite another Bester story, has telepathy. We go along with that. It depends on how good the story is. If the story's good enough, you say, "Sure, they've got teleportation. Now let me see what else has happened." If the story's bad, you say, "Ah, teleportation. Dumb idea. Ridiculous." And you put the book down. But you don't really put it down because of the implausibility of the science of paranormal phenomena. You put it down because the story is not very good. And that's a legitimate reason for putting it any story down.

Q: How do you respond to Hal Clement's famous statement that the difference between science fiction and mainstream fiction is that science fiction has higher standards of realism?

Sheffield: I agree. Science fiction includes all possible universes. Therefore any other fiction is a subset. At its best, science fiction, because it has more potential than any other field of fiction, will be superior. At its worst . . . Well, we've all read it at its worst . . . although some of the best stories are badly written. One of the unusual things about science fiction is that if you come up with a really good idea, you can get away with things which, in other fields of literature, you'd be hanged for doing. You can commit literary anathema and get away with it, precisely because of the interesting idea. Many readers will still love you.

Q: What are you working on now?

Sheffield: At the moment I am finishing this book on the borderlands of science and science fiction. I am also writing another Jupiter™ book—the name of the series—called *The Cyborg from Earth*. When I've finished that, I'll write a big book called *Aftermath,* which takes place after a supernova has exploded had grave effects on the Earth. It's a disaster novel set at a peculiar time. When a supernova explodes, first you get a big flash of light — the visible radiation and the x-rays. Then you get slower-than-light, energetic particles that follow up. They will zap the world in different and worse ways than the visible radiation, but much later. The book is set in the interim period.

Q: Thank you, Charles.

SUSAN SHWARTZ

Q: A great deal of your fiction, including your recently published novel, *Shards of Empire,* is informed by a strong sense of history. So I suppose the obvious place to start is discussing the fantasy aspects of the fantasy-historical novel. These could presumably have been straight, realistic historical novels. Why are they not? What is the special use for fantasy in conjunction with history?

Shwartz: The historical fantasy story is one in which, as with all fantasies, there is magic and the magic works and should drive the action of the plot in the sense that the science drives the action in a classic science-fiction plot. The reason that they are historical fantasies rather than straight historicals is that the magic is magic derived from the actual time in which I am writing. For example, in the eleventh-century setting of *Shards of Empire,* I'm dealing with esoteric Christianity. I'm dealing with esoteric Judaism. Because I am—or my story is—in Anatolia and Cappadocia—I visited there—it's an area in which the ancient magic and religion is very close to the surface, like in Arslan near Hattusas, Hittite things, the leopard-goddess from Catal-Höyuk. When I was over there, I thought, *Oh boy, this is useful stuff. I can write about this.* But the thing is that, for the magic to be effective in a historical fantasy, it must be magic that's derived from the period in which I'm working.

Q: I think that the historical period also has to resonate with the plot. So, do you pick a historical period and then construct a story set in it, or do you pick a historical period which fits the plot you have in mind?

Shwartz: Actually what I do is wait until alarm bells and fireworks go off inside my head, and I think *that's neat. I really, really like that.* And I never know what's going to start me off with that reaction. It could be seeing something. It could be going someplace. It could be an artifact. There was a necklace—amethyst, freshwater pearls, and aquamarines at the Metropolitan Museum in New York—which belonged to a Byzantine princess, and the princess materialized and said, "I think you ought to buy this," which I didn't, and "I think you ought to write about me," which I did.

Or it could be something in a vacation that says, "Oh, wow, this would certainly make a good book."

Q: For *Shards of Empire,* you went to Turkey and found a bunch of things.

Shwartz: I had always wanted to go there. I had written books set in a kind of alternative Egypto-Byzantine Empire, and then *Silk Roads and Shadows* was ninth century, so I wound up in Turkey, and I went down to Cappadocia, and I had not seen the cave-cities. I had really not even heard about them, and I was in there, about nine levels underground. I looked at my guide—because I was traveling with a guide and driver—and I looked up the air-shaft and said, "If I were invading, how would you take one of these?" And Ali, my guide, looked at me and must have thought, *Oh my gosh, the American lady novelist is nuts.* And I said, "It's all right. I write novels. And we started figuring out how one would capture one of these. I looked for a sort of nexus event, and what I came up with was the disastrous late-eleventh-century battle of Manzikert where an emperor was taken prisoner. It was, essentially, where the dike burst, and the Turks who had been coming into the Byzantine Empire now were able to flood into Anatolia. The Byzantines themselves knew it was the beginning of the end. They referred to it as "that dreadful day."

I wanted to see what was happening as a result of it, and the battle was lost because of treachery, so I thought, well, let's put somebody close to this who witnesses it, and see what we can come up with. The rest of it was Richard Curtis's fault, because he said he wanted to see something about the Jews of Byzantium. So I did.

Q: We get back to the original question: why not a straight historical novel about the Jews of Byzantium?

Shwartz: Because I wanted the magic. It sounds kind of strange, but I'm an English medievalist. I grew up in the American Midwest. I live in New York. Nevertheless, I got to Istanbul, and the place just felt right. Five thousand years back, maybe, I was a Middle Easterner or Near Easterner. I just felt very comfortable there. The resonances were good, and something was talking to me, and when something is talking to me, I'm not talking analytically.

Q: I think that in a sense a historical fantasy is more realistic than a straight historical novel, because the people of the time clearly believed in the everyday reality of magic and the supernatural, and to not include this in the novel would be to impose a twentieth-century sensibility on the material.

Shwartz: I think you're absolutely right. Byzantium was not a secular culture. Eleventh-century Turkestan, if you can call it that, and eleventh-century Persia, were not secular societies. Earlier societies did see powers about them. So this doesn't trouble me one single bit. I think of how in our mechanistic age, we nevertheless read horoscopes and check our fortune-cookies and indulge in magical activities like salt pouring over your shoulder and knock wood. That, as you say, makes a difference.

Q: I suppose that an eleventh-century reader would say, "Oh yes, things like that happen. This is a realistic narrative."

Shwartz: I wouldn't go so far as to say that. I'm telling a story. What I try to do is create an illusion of period. I'm not there. I've never been there. I'd never be there back in the eleventh century and I probably wouldn't survive even if I went back there. So what I have to do is create an illusion which the reader finds intellectually satisfying and emotionally resonant.

Q: Does your research then determine what comes in the story, or does the story then direct you to do research to find something that fits?

Shwartz: I like researching. Research is what I do so I can avoid writing. Research is what I was trained to do. What I did for *Shards* and for *Cross and Crescent* (which is the working title for the book that follows it on the First Crusade) was get access to the Center of Byzantine Studies at Dumbarton Oaks in Washington, D.C. Basically what I did was go down there and look at the artifacts and start reading the books, the primary texts in translation, of the period. I knew which area I wanted to work in. I knew I wanted to do the Battle of Manzikert, so I read everything I could about the Battle of Manzikert. I knew I was dealing with the Jews of Byzantium, so I was reading what I could find there, and I was hoping that I would eventually do enough research that things would start to emerge from the pattern.

Well, I found out some interesting things about the Jews' position in Byzantine canon law. There were laws against intermarriage, which means it probably happened pretty often. I found out very interesting things about the culture. I was reading about Cappadocia. And then I took a look about the emperor about whom I was writing, Diogenes Romanus IV, who I knew was blinded out in Kutahya, which is a pottery center now; and saw that he wasn't just blinded by imperial soldiers. They drafted a Jewish merchant. This is the sort of thing you look at and say, "Oh my. I can use this. I'm going to steal it." If you do enough research and you do it right, sooner or later, the research is going to tell the story for you. You can't make these things up. You have to find them.

Q: I suppose this gives you a sense of humility to realize that there are things better than what you can imagine.

Shwartz: Me, I'm just a magpie. I pick 'em up. I don't even feel the humility because I'm too busy being delighted, and I'm also scared. Can I pull this off? Can I get this effect right? Can I make this emotionally convincing?

I set myself a rough task in *Shards of Empire* because I was dealing with an eleventh-century man who had the equivalent of Post-Traumatic Stress Disorder in our own century. And I knew from a book by Dr. Shays, *Achilles in Vietnam,* what the symptomatology of that is in a Vietnam veteran, and I wanted to try to take it back into Byzantium and see the effects of how a particularly treacherous defeat worked on a sensitive man who was a reluctant fighter. It was kind of an interesting thing to do. I was afraid of it. I was also concerned about doing what is really a massed set of cavalry charges and creating not just the effect but the emotion and making it convincing enough so that a veteran might not look at it and say, "Oh my God, lady, tend to your knitting," or something sexist like that. And I did it.

Q: Were you able to find any first-hand accounts by somebody who had actually fought the battle and could tell you what it was like to be there?

Shwartz: Harry Turtledove was kind enough to let me use his translation of Attalietes, who served under Diogenes Romanus, who fancied himself, and was, a good military historian. The Byzantines tended to produce good ones. Attalietes was an eyewitness, and he was on Romanus's side. So I did get to use this. For the rest of it, Michael Psellus wasn't there. Anna Comnena certainly wasn't there. She was much later, but she would have spoken to veterans of the war, and her sources are usually quite good for military history.

Q: I should think that what the novelist would be looking for at this point would be someone who could tell you what the camp routine was like, what it felt like to wear the armor, and what they ate for breakfast, and what the soldiers complained about.

Shwartz: You have things like that in the Byzantine History library. I used the *Strategicon* of Maurice. I used Leo's *Tactics*. I used Nicephorus Phocas's *On Shadow Warfare*. They have all these things codified and laid down. The Byzantines were great paymasters. The Byzantine armies were excellent ones, although they fell on very hard times, and this was one of the times in which they were in some disarray. The coinage was in bad shape and they weren't paying. So they got desertions. Also they had brought in, as the western Romans did, a lot of federates, a lot of Turks, in fact. A lot of Norman mercenaries; and Byzantines always had trouble with Norman mercenaries, even though their own works, like the *Strategicon* of Maurice laid down how you deal with the Celts, how you deal with this group of people, with that group of people—they all come under the heading of *barbaroi*, barbarians or outlanders. The Byzantines studied them quite pragmatically and figured out how to exploit them.

Q: I've encountered historians who say that, basically, there's no substitute for bad generalship. Romanus screwed it up.

Shwartz: Romanus didn't screw it up. He made some bad moves. But, at some point he was at least a competent general. I was reading Trevor Depuy, and Depuy says what they needed really as a man of genius, which Romanus wasn't. He was a general who was good enough. He had always been good enough. But he was up against a general who was better than he, Alp Arslan, and his Persians. Also, no general is proof against the treason of his second in command, which is what happened to Romanus.

Q: He did let himself get suckered into an over-extended charge all the way across the field. I believe that the manuals said never do that against Turks.

Shwartz: No, you never do that against Turks because the Turks will always draw back, and then they'll come and get you, and their aim is very good. And he left his camp unguarded, but it seemed like a reasonable thing to do at the time, and it seemed to me from my own reading of the battle that he was winning. He did make some make some mistakes, but they were not mistakes that were irrevocable, and if he had been able to bring up the second line, the rear guard, I think he probably would have won the day. Alp Arslan did ask for terms. This was a feint, of course, but he did ask. I think, at the very least, Romanus had a fighting chance, if he hadn't been betrayed.

Q: This is how you get into alternate history, wondering what would have happened if it had gone the other way, as in your own series of novels based on the premise that Antony and Cleopatra won at Actium. What special appeal do you find in this kind of writing?

Shwartz: It's a game. For me it's one of the most absorbing mental disciplines I've ever found. It's a lot of fun. You take a point in history and you work it the other way. I've written a number of shorter pieces on this. You get to play with characters who lost and make them out to be winners. You get to change the background.

For example, I did a story that was a Nebula nominee, called

"Loose Cannon" in *Alternate Heroes*. I've always been fascinated with Lawrence of Arabia, who died in 1935 in a motorcycle crash. At the time there were rumors. Churchill had always favored Lawrence. Churchill was very interested in bringing him forward again, although he'd retired from the tank corps and from the R.A.F., and it was '35. After the crash, there were rumors that the Germans had caused it. I know it was a wild rumor. But my premise was that he survived. He didn't have that shattered head. Churchill had him patched together both physically and mentally. I gave him what the British would call an alienist — a psychoanalyst — Ernest Jones, who was a Freudian scholar and literary critic, and they put him back together. So I begin my story "Loose Cannon" — which is a good description of Lawrence — in the middle of the Battle of Britain. A cathedral has been hit. Somebody has been caught under a beam, and a small man limps over and, with unusual strength, pries the guy out. The man who has been rescued looks at him and says, "Don't I know you?" "No." And someone comes up and says, "Colonel, they're waiting for you at Number 10." I got the image for this story, not just from my fascination with Lawrence, but the image of the beleaguered St. Paul's Cathedral during the Blitz.

Q: I think this is what we're looking for in such stories. Some alternate histories are just elaborate games—rearranging the pieces like Scrabble tiles—but the best stories come from such images, which resonate deeply.

Shwartz: Another story I did, and I suppose it's the most powerful I've written, is "Suppose They Gave a Peace." It was up for the Nebula and Hugo and was in Resnick's *Alternate Presidents*. That story was the most deeply meaningful to me, because it concerned my own activism against the Vietnam War. When I started college, a boy who had been the paperboy on my street was killed by friendly fire, and my mother told about going over there with the flag. Another young man on that street came back in very, very bad shape.

This always spoke to me. I am a person who went from being a pacifist to a person who reads one heck of a lot of military history and talks with veterans a lot. A lot of my life has been spent trying to look at this scourge of war that we don't seem to be able to shake and probably that we are not going to be able to shake, and I'm trying to come to terms with it. I told this story in a first-person voice singular that was my father's voice, and I told the story of an Ohio lawyer who is coming home and sees that the military car is outside his house. He has—or had—a son who is a Marine. He has a daughter who is a political activist. He has a world in flux. And I tried to tell this one. This was very much the way my life was, although I had no brother. My father was an army captain and a veteran of the Battle of the Bulge. It was always hard to square my father's own silent pride in his service and my own pride in his ability to protect us against Nazis, since I'm Jewish, with my own utter opposition to the Vietnam war. A lot of what I'm writing is a meditation on war. I'm not comfortable with doing this, but, on the other hand, I don't think the writing particularly gives a damn if I'm comfortable or not.

Q: If you were utterly comfortable, the writing would lose its edge.

Shwartz: It wouldn't be anything I'd want to read. It would be fuzzy and derivative. Writing, to a great extent, is conflict, conflict among characters, conflict in situation, someone being conflicted with his or her role. I can write funny. I can write joyous. *Shards of Empire* was, in some ways, one of the easiest books for me to write because my characters gave me no resistance. Now in *The Grail of Hearts,* they fought me like a son-of-a-gun.

Q: You've also collaborated with other writers. How did your collaboration with Andre Norton come about?

Shwartz: Andre saw my book, *Silk Roads and Shadows.* Andre, unbeknownst to me, had been studying China and the Silk Road for twenty or thirty years, and she wrote the story of Chao Chun, who was an adoptive princess in the Han Dynasty, who married the heir to the ruler of the Hsiung-nu and went out into western China, into what is now the Uighur Autonomous Republic, which is also a great, howling wilderness.

So Andre suggested a collaboration, and didn't I want to come down and work with all her marvelous research materials? I couldn't get there fast enough.

Q: So here you are collaborating with this legendary figure whose work most of us grew up reading. What happens next? Does she give you an outline of the proposed story or do you give her a draft, or what?

Shwartz: Andre tells me what she wants to do, and I say, "Yes, that's interesting. What about this. What about that?" We bat it back and forth. We evolve a proposal and then we go off and we work on it. I'll usually produce most of a first draft, and then she shows me how it really should be done. She is a senior pro; and the tricks of the trade that a senior pro does effortlessly are really an education in themselves for me.

Q: So, what are you doing now?

Shwartz: I just turned in a very large historical fantasy. It's set about 25 years after *Shards of Empire* begins, about the time that the news got out of the Rhineland massacres, which is what they started out with in the First Crusade before they even got to the Middle East. I start out with the Byzantines and the Byzantine Jews finding out that they're getting the Normans coming over with all the westerners. They're here. There goes the neighborhood. It's going to get worse. I deal with some of the characters from *Shards of Empire* and, basically, I go through the First Crusade.

Josepha Sherman and I are writing a *Star Trek* novel in the Classic Trek series, focusing mostly on Mr. Spock, and I am researching around and waiting for something to come and talk to me and grab me.

Q: Thank you, Susan.

MICHAEL SWANWICK

Q: *The Iron Dragon's Daughter* certainly represents a new direction for you. What made you turn to fantasy just now?

Swanwick: I've always loved fantasy. It was my first love. I was sixteen when I read *The Lord of the Rings*. My sister Patty had sent home from college a box of paperbacks she was done with and among them was *The Fellowship of the Ring*. I finished my homework about eleven-thirty, and thought I'd read a chapter or two before bed. By one o'clock I'd given up all hope of sleep and was intent on finishing the book before classes started. I had to skip breakfast to do it, but by God I read the last page just as they opened the school doors. A kind of madness overcame me; I sought out all the fantasy there was in print at the time. But that was the Sixties, and there wasn't much fantasy in print. So I started reading science fiction, because it had a fantasy-like flavor, and by a process of displacement my loyalties shifted.

Q: And of course *The Iron Dragon's Daughter* is a very science-fiction-flavored fantasy. How different do you think your career would have been if you had gone into fantasy immediately?

Swanwick: I probably would have written some extremely dreadful fantasy. [Laughs.] I can't imagine my career being markedly different. Writing a fantasy novel, though, I discovered that science fiction and fantasy are entirely different things. The big difference is that science fiction is set in a knowable universe, and fantasy is set in a universe that, at heart, is unknowable. In science fiction, the characters may not be able to comprehend the universe, but it is at least potentially comprehensible by someone or something with a large enough intelligence and access to the right information. In fantasy, you're treading in God territory.

Q: What impresses me about the book is that the imagery is modern. Elfland has kept pace with the times, as indeed it did in folklore. The various Elflands of the past reflect the human world of the same era. The Elfland of Shakespeare's *A Midsummer Night's Dream* reflects Tudor England. Yours has shopping malls and elves in pin-stripe suits. Somehow the book makes itself more real that way, rather than increasingly contrived. So, how does one touch the real amid the fantastic?

Swanwick: The reflection of the real world is what made it worth doing. The modern elements didn't make the fantasy more difficult to write—quite the opposite. Years ago when I was driving through Ireland, I turned a corner on a road and there through a break in the trees was Newgrange. I had to pull the rental car over, I was laughing so hard. Because Newgrange, which is a very famous neolithic chambered cairn, was at the same time awesome and whimsical. It looked like it had been built by a race of conqueror hobbits! Everything I saw in Ireland—and later Scotland—was like that. Either larger or smaller than I expected. Weird in ways I wasn't prepared for. Even castles were nothing like I'd imagined. It struck me that Americans were at a disadvantage writing fantasy because we hadn't grown up with stone rings and Roman roads running through our backyards. We didn't know what they were like. We hadn't had any evocative experiences in such places. Which leaves us writing fiction based not on our own experiences and perceptions but on other people's books. So when I came up with a mechanism for including factories and go-go bars and high school shop classes, this gave the fiction a powerful boost because I could more readily see and imagine the places and therefore the people within them. As a bonus I discovered that when you use elves and fairies as metaphors for people you know . . . this makes them comprehensible in ways they otherwise are not. In real life you are constantly being mystified by

people and their behavior . . . but once you say they're all elves
and gnomes and similarly irrational creatures, all of a sudden
their actions become comprehensible in a way they're just not
in the regular world.

Q: They become comprehensible by being incomprehensible?

Swanwick: They're more understandable. You're exempted
from the obligation to provide the sort of pat psychological
explanations that fiction routinely proffers up but that you
never experience in with real people—even with yourself, actually. People in action are mysterious and the metaphor
preserves that mystery.

Q: Is this a revelation, or an excuse?

Swanwick: A little bit of both.

Q: You've mentioned elsewhere that you think that the
publishing climate is right for literarily ambitious fantasy, as
opposed to more Tolkien clones. Why do you think this is so?

Swanwick: I think it's been right for a long time. Fantasy is
an incredibly rich field. I've been amazed that so few writers
have taken full advantage of its possibilities. Through the '70s
and '80s there was an enormous expansion of the market and
influx of new writers. Yet we never saw the kind of literary
in-fighting and grouping and the clashes that we saw in science
fiction, or in horror, for that matter, where people were always
locking horns because what they did literarily meant so much
to them. What we got were by and large books that were not at
all ambitious, that were just another fantasy trilogy quest for
the enchanted sword or sacred cup or magic corkscrew. I am not
indicting all fantasy trilogy quests here, but we have all read
too many that are identical and interchangeable. For over a
decade I have been saying that it would come, and in the last
couple of years I've seen it—a flowering of ambition. I think
there's going to be markedly more of it in the future.

Q: I wonder if it wasn't a matter of market and editorial influences *holding the writers back*. Do you have any sense that you
were hunkered down in science fiction until the climate in
fantasy became safer for ambitious work?

Swanwick: I don't want to imply that I was waiting for the
fantasy field to be good enough for me—I was waiting for an
idea good enough to support a fantasy novel. But consider the

case of Rachel Pollack whose drop-dead brilliant *Unquench-able Fire* won the British Fantasy Award several years back but was ignored by all the major American houses. Recently, though, there are a lot of fantasists doing major work. Robert Holdstock is a writer who has been around since forever but never really got any recognition until *Mythago Wood* and its sequels exploded into the genre consciousness. Not long ago Greer Ilene Gilman's *Moonwise* simply couldn't have been published. Now there are people like Mary Gentle, James Blaylock, Geoff Ryman—even Rachel Pollack's *Temporary Agency*, which is if anything even better than its precursor, was able to find an American publisher. All these books are coming out. It's the right time for it. I don't know why it wasn't the right time ten or fifteen years ago—and of course there were exceptions then, people like John Crowley, Mike Ford, and so on—but now the sluice gates are open. Twenty years from now people are going to look back on this period with nostalgia and envy.

Q: Maybe the generic book-product has actually become exhausted. More likely, it's being moved away into a separate category by itself, as typified by the *Dragonlance* books. Generic series fantasy is packaged very differently from, say, a novel by Ellen Kushner. It's even put a different part of the bookstore.

Swanwick: Generic, category fiction is not in and of itself evil. My eleven-year-old son loves *Dragonlance* books. It's just not what I aspire to or particularly value. But there is no reason why the existence of ambitious, literary fantasy should threaten people who are writing *Dragonlance,* or vice-versa. The warm reception given to a fairly predictable product doesn't mean you can't go write something like Terry Bisson's *Talking Man,* which is a very different book, selling to a very different audience.

Q: I think the problem is that publishers' sales forces are afraid that a book like *Talking Man* isn't going to sell as well as *The Sword of Shannara.* It is a less predictable product.

Swanwick: That's true, but how many books do sell that well? Whatever number it is, they're publishing them already. They've got some extra marketing slots, so they might as well do some books that will sell less heatedly but steadily, reliably, over the next hundred years or so.

Q: I think you have a more optimistic view of mass-market publishing than I do. Do you feel free to write more fantasy now, to move back into science fiction, or what?

Swanwick: [Laughs.] All of the above.

Q: Okay then, let's talk about your beginnings. How long were you trying to write before you actually sold anything?

Swanwick: I committed myself to writing when I was seventeen. I was working on the loading dock in a furniture factory in Roanoke, Virginia. It was a very dull job. Every five or ten minutes a piece of living room furniture would rattle slowly down a long wooden conveyor belt. My job was to put a large plastic baggie over it—they came in two sizes, chair and sofa—read the tag, and slide it into the proper loading slot. I wasn't allowed to sit down or read or anything between chairs. I had to look busy. So I would walk around this large, featureless building looking at the air, and I'd pick up little scraps of brown paper packing tape and write things on them. I would invent words like "lourish" or "flauvant" or write sentence fragments. By the end of that summer I had worked my way up to entire paragraphs, and decided that was it. I was going to be a writer. I then proceeded to trash my life and prevent myself from acquiring any marketable skills whatsoever so that I would have no choice *but* to be a writer. I wrote steadily for eleven years before I finally finished a story. When I sold my first story, I was twenty-nine years old. In retrospect, I could have done quite nicely with a decent job, maybe a little money; it was a bad career strategy. Kids—don't try this at home!

Q: Why did you have so much trouble finishing a story?

Swanwick: I don't know. Lack of concentration, maybe. Possibly because I had no idea what a story was like. I was trying to be experimental, trying for something not only far beyond anything I could write, but far beyond anything that could be published, maybe even beyond what could be written at all. I look back now on myself struggling to become a writer, and I can see no discernable promise whatsoever. I was just lucky in that in the long run I was capable of learning the craft.

Q: The Greek term is *hubris* . . . But once you started selling, you succeeded quite quickly. Did you not have two out of your first three stories on the Nebula ballot?

Swanwick: That was actually fortunate: the first one got held up for several years. The place that bought it, regretted it. They published it in an anthology of stories that they wished they hadn't bought. Eileen Gunn was also in that anthology; she had the only good story in the book. But as a result I was able to brag that my first two published works had been nominated. The glow of that kept me going about ten years.

Q: What anthology was it?

Swanwick: It was called *Proteus: New Voices for the '80s,* edited by Richard McEnroe. The story was originally bought for *Destinies.* Every six months, when a new volume came out, I would rush out, buy it, look through it, and see that my story wasn't there. So I would check each of the stories to see they hadn't accidentally retitled mine and given the credit to Larry Niven or someone like that . . . [laughs] I never did make it into *Destinies.*

Q: But things did progress quickly thereafter. You didn't exactly remain invisible.

Swanwick: I had good luck. Oddly enough, what was probably one of the best pieces of luck was that I *didn't win* any of the awards for my first stories. I've known people who won awards when they were new to the field and then felt they had something to live up to. So every year that went by without another award would be another year of failure. It really soured their relationship with the whole awards process. For me, before I won anything, I had published for ten years. I felt like they'd given me one for just being around for so long. So I was very happy with it. I enjoy watching all the awards, rooting for my favorites, and being disappointed when something that I didn't like beats out something that I liked quite a lot. If one of my first three stories had won, I might not have this pleasure.

Q: How important are awards, as opposed to writing the work?

Swanwick: Oh, they're nice. They're fun to get. They're even fun to lose. Having gotten one, now, I can say that with a clean conscience. You know this yourself, Darrell. When you lose, you go to the party afterwards and all your friends come up to you and they tell you that you were cheated; you should have won; and you get this great outpouring of warmth and camaraderie from people that you care about. You're very careful not to point out that if all these people had actually voted you for the award you *would* have won . . . [Laughs.] Awards are fun, but mostly for the social aspect. Though there's no denying the effect they can have on your career.

Q: You might even sell books. I know from experience that publishers like to be able to put "Podunk Award Winner" on the book cover. It almost doesn't matter *what* award it is. This will actually make the buyers from the big chains order more copies. If you don't have any real awards, an particularly imaginative publisher might *invent* something to put on the cover.

Swanwick: When I won the Nebula, Bill Gibson called me up and said the single best thing I've ever heard about awards. He said, "Now that you've won it, you need never want one again. That little tag, Nebula Award winner' will follow you around for the rest of your life. Winning fifty more isn't going to change it at all. It's never going to go away. They can't take it away from you. For the rest of your life, you need never want the Nebula again." I thought that was wonderful. He called me up out of nowhere just to free me from the desire for awards.

Q: I bet you wouldn't mind it saying "Fifty-time Nebula Award winner" on the cover, now, would you?

Swanwick: I wouldn't mind. But then, look at Robert Silverberg's books. They never mention the number, and who can keep track of how many he's won? He's just "Hugo and Nebula Award-winner Robert Silverberg."

Q: I suppose the other artificiality other than awards is literary movements. You came into science fiction when Cyberpunk was hot. They were trying to either draft you into that or into something else. Was this at all meaningful?

Swanwick: The first fan letter I ever got was from someone who wanted to know if I thought that there was any replacement for the New Wave. I told him no. Cyberpunk came up about a year later. There is always a position in science fiction for the loyal opposition. If you've got a couple of talented writers, and you only need a couple, you can claim your right as the pretender to the throne to sit in the Siege Perilous and you can draw lightning from the sky. You get all the attention and all the madness and you challenge everybody, and you have them arguing over whether you have talent or not. It's very easy to do. I am amazed that more people don't do this. We're ripe for another such movement right now, in fact. The controversies provide a lot of heat and hurt feelings, but when they die down that's all forgotten. All that remains of cyberpunk today is some interesting literary criticism, the works of Gibson, Sterling, Cadigan, a few others. That's enough.

Q: I am reminded of Brian Aldiss's comment that the New Wave was a publicity stunt.

Swanwick: Ah, but a good one. I loved the New Wave. To me, that is the golden age of science fiction. They were coming out with such wonderful things as the *Quark* series, which Delany and Hacker edited. Harlan Ellison was writing some of his best stuff then. Moorcock, Priest, Ballard, Disch, Aldiss were all in peak form. There were tons and tons and tons of good things: *Barefoot in the Head,* one of my favorite novels, was being excerpted here and there. It was a very exciting, very productive time of literary ferment. I don't think it was just publicity, but whatever people are talking about obsessively will turn into publicity. The works themselves, I think, did a lot for science fiction.

Q: It may have been more the *idea* of such works than the works themselves. If you go back and reread *New Worlds* from the '60s, rather than reading just the famous works from those issues that we remember, like *Camp Concentration* and *Barefoot in the Head,* you'll find that some of the material is painfully bad. It's the worst anyone has ever seen. I think what happened was that all rules were suspended. So someone could proclaim himself a revolutionary and use this as an excuse for having nothing to say. So there was a down-side of the New Wave too.

Swanwick: I was on the Nebula jury off and on for years, and when you read *everything* that's printed in the field in a given year, you discover that there is not a lot that is terribly good. There is far less than you would think. You lose proportion and get excited about stories that are merely well written. I was constantly raving about stories that Marianne would read and not be particularly moved by. Marianne Porter, my wife, is a more typical science fiction reader. She pretty much expects top-of-the-line when she reads. Stories that are good enough to win awards. That's what she enjoys. Most science fiction most of the time isn't all that good. But the bad goes away on its own, and it only takes a handful of stories to create a time in the field that in retrospect looks pretty good.

Q: How did all that massive reading effect you as a writer? How did you avoid becoming hideously in-bred, in a literary sense, that is?

Swanwick: Two years of jury service is about the maximum amount of time you can do it. Then you have to go away and read a lot elsewhere, folks like A.S. Byatt and Tony Hillerman and Cecelia Holland and Vladimir Nabokov, until your hands stop twitching. And of course you have to do a lot of wandering around, talking to people, having encounters with maniacs and murderers and street sweepers, and so on. The advantage of being on the jury was the exchange of letters. Holding a literary correspondence with people like Gardner Dozois and Terry Carr, arguing the merits of individual works with people who knew the field so well, was an educational experience unlike any other. The disadvantage . . . When I was on the jury I came home one day to find the Post Office had been there and UPS and Federal Express, and there was a *mound* of packages of books awaiting me. I stacked them up on the kitchen table, and piled that way, they towered over me. Then I added up the face value of all the books. It came to something like $187.45 . . . I thought, *Wow!* I just got $187.45 worth of science fiction *free.* Then I realized: *Now I have to read it.* It was the first time in my life that I'd ever had more science fiction in front of me than I wanted to read. It was a shattering moment for me. I think that was when I gave up being on the jury. I couldn't do it anymore.

Q: Do you find that what you read has an immediately discernable influence on what you write?

Swanwick: No. Everything goes in and gets filtered through the subconscious, and it comes out again years later. I am constantly recognizing people that I met or stories that I read ten or fifteen years ago, things I was thinking about a long time ago. For me, it all goes through the hind-brain. There's the occasional exception. In Kim Stanley Robinson's story "Black Air"—a terrific story about a boy on the Spanish Armada having various visions and hallucinations—there was a wonderful scene where St. Elmo's Fire covers the masts and the boy dances up among the *fata morganas*. I read that when I was right in the middle of writing a story set in a church, and loved the image so much I decided to steal it on the spot. So during a lightning storm my character goes inside the church organ—there are ladders inside, you can climb up within it—and dances around up there with the fata morganas. But that's rare. Usually by the time an influence comes out, it's been so transformed only I can recognize it.

Q: What story of yours are you describing?

Swanwick: It was called "Covenant of Souls." I was working for Tabernacle Church in West Philly as a church secretary. I came in early one day, about twenty minutes before work started, and decided as an exercise to write ten opening lines. When I got to the fourth, "Something ugly was growing in the air over the altar," I liked that one so much that I wrote the next sentence, and then the next paragraph. The story came right out of nowhere. This is not at all the way I write. I usually know how the story is going to end before I begin it. But in this story, I had no idea what was going on. I was writing it, slowly and painfully, but steadily. I could feel it all adding up to something. There was somebody living in the dirt basement under the sanctuary, and she would come out at night and climb into the children's nursery and eat all the crayons. A government man, who is possibly a robot, comes and asks threatening questions. Street people move onto the lawn and begin roasting dogs in the window wells and having revival meetings. The protagonist, who was not me but had the same job as I had, realizes that something wrong is going on, something strange. He drops acid. And I could see that all this was leading up to something. I am enough of a writer to see the little hints and foreshadowings I was very carefully laying down. But I had no idea what was going on. I turned to Gardner Dozois and Jack Dann and asked their advice. They're both terrific story-doctors. They both said, "Keep writing," which at the time did not seem like much help. But I kept writing until about two-thirds of the way through, when suddenly my son was born. Everything snapped into place, and I understood it was all about the fears my conscious mind couldn't express, having a baby on the way. It's a very common phenomenon for expectant parents to have nightmares of monsters clawing their way out of the womb and the like. The woman eating crayons is a classic example of pica, the irrational food cravings a pregnant woman can have. And so on. Once I realized that, it all fell into place. It was all about the fears parents have for their unborn children. And then of course I knew how to end it.

Q: To what extent do you think that your science fiction novels reflect ideas that are current, just in the air of the field? *Vacuum Flowers* is very different, but it certainly reflects ideas that John Varley had previous explored.

Swanwick: A lot does come that way. If you're involved in science fiction, what people are writing about and talking about and arguing about, is a good guide to where the intellectual action is. Also, we're all responding to real developments in science. There was a time, about twenty years ago, just before home computers came along, when everybody was writing about computers. Nobody could write a story set in the future without accounting for what happens to computers. Now, they're taken so for granted that they can just be absorbed into the background. Today the question you have to deal with is virtual reality. What are you going to do with virtual reality, and to a lesser degree, nanotechnology? When I wrote *Stations of the Tide,* one big concern, when dealing with a far future and a very technologically-advanced future—it was forced into my hand that I had to deal with a version of virtual reality. I worked extremely hard to make my version different from William Gibson's, so I wouldn't be ripping him off. He had this single, overwhelming vision that swallowed everybody else's up. It was so natural and so compelling that everybody assumed it was common property and they were entitled to use it. I worked very hard not to, to be different. The version I came up with is sort of like cyberspace after a century or so has passed and the Republicans have regained control.

Q: Maybe Ronald Reagan was a technological simulacrum.

Swanwick: Indeed, who among us has ever met him?

Q: At this point the established, mainstream critics would insist that SF is hopelessly in-bred and incestuous, addressing just itself rather than eternal verities. But you could argue that all literature is an on-going dialogue, in the sense that Elizabethan theater began with Marlowe and a few others, and later everybody was answering Shakespeare. Is this so, or is science fiction curiously and uniquely self-referential?

Swanwick: I think you're absolutely right. But it's not just that we're engaged in a conversation for its own sake—we are, but we've all had the experience that we say much more interesting and intelligent things in arguments than just sitting around mumbling to ourselves. The opposition of other voices, the skepticism they may bring to anything you might say, and their willingness to take and amplify your thoughts, raises the level of discourse to a much higher plane. This shows when somebody who does not read science fiction tries to write it. They write these dreadful stories where people are living in domed cities, and outside there is pure anarchy and people living in the radioactive wilderness. It's totally implausible fiction based on ideas that were old thirty or forty years ago. But these writers have nobody to talk to who can understand the way things break down and the way technology develops. You're much better off having the *Analog* crew around. You get much better literature when you can sit around and talk with them. When you know that somebody like Charles Sheffield or Mike Flynn might be reading your story, someone who knows what is and is not possible technologically, you're more willing to put in the hard thought it takes to avoid their scorn.

Q: This can also make stories date. The Technocracy Movement was a serious movement in the 1930's, sort of the way Libertarianism is today. There were stories about it. Now it's a historical footnote. Those stories are much less meaningful today. So, don't stories run the danger of becoming fossilizations of what we were talking about twenty years ago? There may be some limitations to the topical approach.

Swanwick: Topicality isn't all that is going on. But at the same time I think that all serious literature dates itself almost immediately. Toward the end of Modernism, what the people who are called the K-Mart Realists were reacting against, they had a set of conventions in which you had a background world that was smooth and glossy and without identifiable features. You went to the store; you never went to K-Mart. The world was sketchily drawn with as few specific details as possible. It didn't work. I try to make all my fiction tie into the time well enough that it dates. If it is lasting value, it will last in spite of that, the way Dickens has, and if it is not of lasting value, then it'll be like Norman Mailer. It will just go away.

Q: Who are the K-Mart Realists?

Swanwick: Oh, Ann Beattie, Bobby Ann Mason, I guess Raymond Carver, people like that. When they came along, was when mainstream fiction started to get interesting again. They were dealing with real people rather than playing a literary game, which is what too much of Modernism had devolved into. Good science fiction and fantasy really do engage the real world, perhaps at a strange level and in a strange way, but their claim to literary interest is that they're not just somebody writing uncritically about his own experiences, but a transformation of the real world into metaphor through artifice.

Q: What are you working on now?

Swanwick: Right now, I am working on a story set on the train to Hell. I'm working on a story with Jack Dann called "Ships," which starts immediately after the protagonist dies. In fact, about a month ago I suddenly looked up and realized I was working on three stories at the same time, and that the protagonist in all three was dead. A strange and unnerving message to receive from the unconscious. The third one is "Radio Waves," which I just sold to Ellen Datlow. I started a collaboration with Terry Bisson. He bailed out of it so I wrote it myself and sold it to *Asimov's*. I named the protagonist after him, so he'll have a surprise when he reads that particular issue. And I'm working on a children's book. I'm working on a collaborative novella with Gardner Dozois; two novellas, actually, but one is on the back burner. A zombie story, a hard science story—just to keep my oar in—a planet-sized grasshopper story, maybe a piece of interactive fiction if the software ever comes through. And of course I'm working on my next novel, something far more ambitious than anything I've ever essayed before and probably, God help me, the first volume of a trilogy. I have a lot in the works. We'll see how it comes out.

Q: How do you work on several things at once without finishing one? Many writers would find that enormously difficult.

Swanwick: It is difficult. But when the ideas come along and they're hot, you have to do them or lose them, whether or not you have the time. I'll work on one until it begins to bog down, and then pick up another one. I think all or almost all the projects I am working on now will get finished. At any given time I've got forty stories uncompleted sitting around in my files. The longest of them is eighty pages. The oldest, I started, oh, twenty-eight years ago. Every now and then I'll pick one up and start working on it, and it'll come back to life again. So none of them are necessarily dead. But the ones I am working on right now, I think they're all going to get finished.

Q: Thanks, Michael.

EVANGELINE WALTON

Q: One of the things that's always impressed me about your career is how much sheer patience you must have, to have held out for almost forty years before you suddenly became famous in the 1970s. How did you do it?

Walton: As for patience, I just gritted my teeth and went on. That was all there was to it.

Q: Was it possibly that the world wasn't ready for *The Virgin and the Swine* in 1936?

Walton: I don't know. It seemed like nobody was making a go of fantasy in 1936. My book hit the market the same time *Gone with the Wind* did, and you can imagine how much chance anything had against *Gone with the Wind*.

Q: Had you actually finished the other four Mabinogion books at that time, or were they rewritten or finished later, nearer to when they saw print?

Walton: I wrote them from scratch after *The Virgin and the Swine*. I was still in Indianapolis then. The only book written from scratch in Arizona was *The Cross and the Sword*. I might have finished the other three Mabinogion books in the '30s. I'm not sure now. I know I did the first draft of the Theseus trilogy before World War II was quite over.

Q: You must have had some faith that all this material eventually would be published, however long it took.

Walton: Naturally, while you're at work on a labor of love, anything seems possible. I certainly had enough uncertainties between my sessions at the typewriter. Either a thing is there and has to come out, or it doesn't, I think.

Q: You were certainly fortunate that the material wasn't topical, but instead completely timeless, so, for all one generation of readers got cheated out of reading these books, from the present-day reader's point of view it didn't matter that they took so long to get published.

Walton: Well, my material is what is now considered timeless, thank Heaven. When I first tried to publish it, it was considered all out-of-date.

Q: You mean critics and publishers figured, well, nobody reads Cabell anymore, so nobody will read this stuff?

Walton: Yes. I don't think Cabell read me, though.

Q: My point is that Cabell himself was regarded as very out-of-date by 1939 or so.

Walton: He retired as James Branch Cabell sometime in the '30s. The he appeared as plain Branch Cabell in a few years, and you were supposed to think it was somebody else. That's my recollection of the situation, in any case.

Q: Had you read anybody else's treatment of the Welsh material, such as Kenneth Morris's *Book of the Three Dragons* before you wrote *The Virgin and the Swine* and the others?

Walton: No. At the time I was working on the Mabinogion material, I thought it was still virgin, that nobody else had handled it. I am very glad I didn't know about Kenneth Morris's admirable books until later.

Q: You were presumably mostly familiar with the Lady Guest translation of the *Mabinogion*?

Walton: Oh, yes. That was all I had to work on for a while. I couldn't find any other English translation. Of course she was writing in Victorian times and had to be careful—lady-like in Queen Victoria's sense—and there was a place or two where I wasn't sure what really happened. I could only guess. I had a cousin who was teaching in the New England Conservatory of Music at the time, and he was well acquainted with Harvard. So I sent copies of the debatable passages to him, and he got a translation from Harvard's Professor Robinson.

Q: In such a case of the traditional material being vague or elusive, how much leeway do you give yourself to simply make up what is either missing or implied?

Walton: I don't like to contradict anything positively stated in myth. If there are alternate versions I feel free to choose the one I like best. I also feel free to make any additions that don't contradict the original material.

Q: The Fourth Branch of the *Mabinogion,* which you turned into *The Virgin and the Swine,* is needless to say only a tenth as long as your novel. So, how did you go about fleshing the original material out?

Walton: I read all I could find about matriarchy, notably Briffault's *The Mothers* and Sir John Rhys's *Celtic Folklore.* It was like planting seeds—things somehow just sprouted, and fell into new patterns and shapes. The first Branch, which I did last, was my greatest problem: harder to write, for some reason, than any of the others. It has the modern formula—boy meets girl; boy and girl get split up; boy and girl find each other again-so it should have been the easiest. But somehow it was the hardest. I had never been satisfied with my original treatment, and I didn't want to resurrect it at first, but Ballantine wanted all four Branches, and since they'd been nice about the other three, I thought I really owed it to them.

Q: How did you come to write *Witch House*?

Walton: I had had an extremely unpleasant summer. There was a little growth that had to be removed from one arm, and something went wrong, and they kept having to skin the wound every other day all summer. I couldn't think of anything pleasant. Horror isn't my regular field, but I felt too mauled to write anything else that summer.

Q: Other than the one story in *Weird Tales,* "At the End of the Corridor," you never returned to the horror field after that.

Walton: No. I'm too squeamish to write anything in the modern way, I guess. An attempt to bring *Witch House* back a few years ago didn't work, although it had been in print for thirty-two years after its first publication. I'm too mild for nowadays.

Q: How is it that the British edition is 20,000 words longer than the Arkham House version?

Walton: The British publishers asked me to write that. They said it was too short to sell well in England. At first I couldn't think of what to do. The book seemed complete as it was. So I tore my hair and after a while wrote the twenty-thousand extra words. Hearing that the book wouldn't sell without them was a most convincing argument.

Q: Was the modern paperback the Arkham House text or the British?

Walton: The Arkham House. I still have a few copies around of the British edition. I think the British made a paperback of their own. But I never got hold of that.

Q: Which version do you prefer?

Walton: I still think the original is better structurally. Since I wrote the additions, though, I naturally want people to like them.

Q: What is the news on your Theseus trilogy? Is the rest of it coming out soon?

Walton: I finished the second volume last Sunday. [August 27, 1989—D.S.] There is still a lot of revision to be done. Of course there was a first draft made of all three during World War II, but then I had to move to Arizona under rather trying circumstances. There had been deaths in my family. Then for several years I didn't get back at it. Mary Renault's Theseus books had been published in the meantime; and that meant I had to lay mine away for twenty years. So after that, when I did get back to work on it again, there had been a lot of new archeological discoveries and many old ideas had been exploded. So I had to do the books all over from scratch.

Q: Have you plans for anything beyond the Theseus books?

Walton: Well, I'd like to do a little more, but I'll be eighty-two in November. So it's a toss-up. I suppose I'll be doing well if I get the whole trilogy out in my lifetime.

Q: Do you ever think that if only your books had become successful much earlier, it would have encouraged you to have written more? Or have you written what you were going to anyway?

Walton: Yes to your first question.

Q: Who were your favorite writers, back when you were beginning your career, who might be counted as influences?

Walton: Really my most formative influences were the Celtic

Twilight writers. I was quite crazy about them for a number of years before I went to work on my Mabinogion stuff. At that time I thought the Welsh material was a virgin field, and I didn't think I could dare rival any of my beloved Celtic Twilight writers in Irish mythology, so I never tried to touch that.

Q: Would you now?

Walton: No, I don't think I would. I still cherish my memories of theirs. The characters they drew seemed to me to be the way they ought to be, which would leave me no room for new conceptions.

Q: You mean Lady Gregory's books and the like?

Walton: William Butler Yeats and especially James Stephens. James Stephens used to be my bible. I know that when I was working on the proofs of my first book I came across a sentence that I was sure I had unintentionally borrowed from him. So that held the proofs up for three days, while I hunted up said sentence, for three days. I had to think of something else. Then the editor told me later that one sentence wouldn't have mattered in the least. I realized I'd made a fool of myself. But for years I couldn't bear to read my beloved Stephens again. After all this frenzied cramming, I was fed up on him.

Q: Did you read Lord Dunsany?

Walton: I can't think how I came to forget him, because I loved his style. Of course I like mythological subject matter better, but Dunsany's style is unique.

Q: Have you ever wanted to write American material?

Walton: I'm afraid I haven't got any gift for it. I seem to have to go back two or three thousand years.

Q: Can you tell us anything about the new Theseus book?

Walton: It's the second one, the one in which I—or rather, he—has the arguments with bulls and snakes. It's the Cretan adventure. The book published in 1983, was about Theseus and the Amazons. It is customary to put the Cretan adventure first in Theseus's life, but a fragment exists of one of Euripides's plays in which the child Hippolytus laments his father's departure for Crete. It seems unlikely that Hippolytus was born before his father met his mother, so I put the Amazon adventure first.

Q: What about the third book?

Walton: Of course I have the World War II first draft of that, which will take a lot of revision, but maybe less than the other two.

Q: Thank you, Evangeline Walton.

GENE WOLFE

Q: You're been writing full time for several years now. How has this changed your perspectives?

Wolfe: I'm not sure that it's really changed my perspective at all, and I think that perhaps it should have. You're supposed to be more professional, more bottom-line oriented, and I don't think I am, because I spent too long writing as an avocation rather than a profession. I still tend to write that way. I think I tend to write as I like rather than what might be commercial.

Q: To do that and to do it for a living—isn't that the definition of success?

Wolfe: Well, it is if you live off it. I just hope I can do well enough at it. Writing is a long-lead-time profession. You write something, and if you're lucky you see it in print in three or four years. So it's going to be a while longer before I know that I'm really making a go of this. I *hope* I am.

Q: If you found you weren't making enough, would you branch out into other areas of writing? Would you novelize *Dune?*

Wolfe: [laughs] That's a dirty crack.

Q: Well, Joan Vinge did precisely that. She wrote the story book of the movie.

Wolfe: I would always do that sort of thing if somebody really wanted it and wanted to pay me a lot of money to do it. I doubt if anyone is ever going to be willing to pay me to write movie novelizations. I don't think I'm that kind of writer, and people sense that I'm not that kind of writer. I would probably do it for the money if I could. I doubt if the matter is ever going to come up. I suspect that if things don't go well, eventually I'll have to take a job at the carwash or whatever. I'll have to go out into some non-writing field—I've been there before—and do that to make a living if I can. I hope it's not going to come to that. I like being a full-time writer. I hope I can continue to turn out enough successful work that I can continue to do what I'm doing now.

Q: You don't seem to be the sort of writer who can be rushed. Your books don't read like that. Are you indeed a very slow writer?

Wolfe: I don't know what very slow is. A page of first draft, typically, takes me a half an hour. I can be rushed in the sense that I can be made to work longer hours in the day than I normally do. I normally start somewhere around eight and stop somewhere around noon. As far as the actual writing is concerned, I try to reserve the afternoons for research and correspondence and that sort of thing. If deadlines get tight, if things get hard, then obviously I'm going to start cutting into afternoon and evening time. I could write ten hours a day if I had to, and I think I could write as well as I do writing four hours a day. But it's exhausting; and it means that the correspondence and the research don't get done, because you've taken up the time that normally should be devoted to them and actually spent it putting words on paper.

Q: *The Book of the New Sun* seems to be something that was slowly and painstakingly done. I can imagine you going over the first four volumes again and again, as well as the upcoming *The Urth of the New Sun,* and adding details. Was it like that?

Wolfe: It was much more a matter of going over it and chopping out details, actually, because I had written in a number of things when I did my original draft of it that either did not work or would have made a long book even longer—*The Urth of the New Sun* is 110,000 words now, which even for me is a long book; as for *The Book of the New Sun* itself, the first four volumes, that is close to a half a million words—and if I had left certain things in that would have made it longer still. So I cut some things out and condensed scenes to try to bring it down to a reasonable limit.

Q: When you started, did you envision a work of such magnitude?

Wolfe: No, not in the least. I always hate to admit this [laughs]—I started it as a novella for **Orbit.** It definitely got out of control. I wrote on it and I realized I was approaching novella length and it was hardly started. So I thought, well, it's a book. So I did it as a book, which was essentially **The Shadow of the Torturer;** and I realized that I was *still* hardly started, so I said, "Aha! It's a trilogy. I should have known." So I went and did it as a trilogy, and I ended up with three volumes of which the third volume was about half again as long as the first two. I knew I couldn't do a trilogy with a 150,000-word third volume, so I split the third volume into two. That was originally going to be called *The Sword of the Autarch.* It became *The Sword of the Lictor* and *The Citadel of the Autarch.* I had a climactic scene with Baldanders in the middle of the original book, and it became the end of *The Sword of the Lictor.* Then I had room to do some additional things that I hadn't had room to do before, like the story contest in the lazarette when Foila and Melito and Hallvard and Loyal To The Group Of Seventeen all tell their stories. That's the sort of thing that went in, and the story that Severian reads to Little Severian at the foot of Mount Typhon.

Q: How much is there in the way of out-takes?

Wolfe: You mean existing? Well, I don't think any of it exists anymore. I've pretty much scratched it out and thrown it away. Of course in the case of splitting that volume, it wasn't a matter of out-takes. It was a matter of building up. In the case of something like *The Urth of the New Sun* there were out-takes, but usually it was a matter of scrubbing sentences and paragraphs here and there which I had intended to develop into something until I saw that there wasn't *room*—unless I was going to do a whole new series, which I didn't want to do. I wanted to settle the matter of bringing the New Sun and the creation of the new Earth.

Q: Could you tell us something about *The Urth of the New Sun?*

Wolfe: It begins ten years after Severian's story in *The Book of the New Sun.* If you've read *The Book of the New Sun* carefully, you know that it's being written just before he leaves to go and bring the New Sun. This is his last act on Earth before he boards the ship and takes off to leave our universe, which is Briah, and enter the universe of the Hierogrimates, which is Yssut. So *The Urth of the New Sun* is the story of what happens to him immediately after he has finished writing *The Book of the New Sun,* in the time-frame of the novel, if you see what I mean. Now what we're skipping is about ten years in which Severian was the Autarch of the Commonwealth—and also Autarch of Earth in the sense that his title gives him a titular rulership over the planet, which he cannot actually exercise.

Q: It seems to me that the document Severian has produced will be remembered in his world not as an autobiography or historical memoir but as a great myth. It will become like Homer's works and might even be the basis for a religion. Is there any sense of this in the sequel?

Wolfe: Oh, yes. First of all, what you say is absolutely true, and that's why Dr. Talos's play, "Eschatology and Genesis," deals with this sort of thing. For example, if you'll look at the beginning of the play [in Chapter XXIV of *The Claw of the Conciliator*], you'll see that the New Sun is listed as one of the characters in the cast. And of course you never get the complete play because Baldanders goes wild and terrifies the audience and gets shot a little bit and breaks up the show. But what you say has happened, and there's a great deal more in *The Urth of the New Sun.* of how it happens and why it happens. You see Severian not only as the New Sun but also as the Conciliator.

Q: I am fascinated by the vaguely historical models in the series. The Commonwealth, for all that it's set in the Southern Hemisphere, reminds me somewhat of Byzantium during one of its four-hundred-year declines, maybe toward the end of the Comnenus period. That is, it is clearly declining and will continue to do so, but it will just as clearly go on well beyond anyone's lifetime. Did you have any of this specifically in mind?

Wolfe: Yes, absolutely. I was very happy to hear you say that, because people look at *The Shadow of the Torturer* and they say, "The Torturers' Guild—Ah, this is Medieval Europe." And it isn't. It's Byzantium, and that's where the model for it comes from. I've gotten a lot of criticism about bad Latin in the books, because to a modern Latinist, Latin is the language of Cicero, and I was using the Latin of, say, about A.D. 1000, late Byzantine Latin, which, from the standpoint of a classicist who is interested in Vergil and that sort of writer, is a corrupt Latin because, although Latin is a dead language now, it was a *living* language for two thousand years or so at least; and it developed. It changed. There is an early Latin, an archaic Latin if you want to call it that. There is the classical Latin which you get when you read the classical Latin poets and dramatists, and there is a Byzantine Latin which is really contemporaneous with the early Middle Ages. We tend to think of the classical world as ending with the sack of Rome, and it simply didn't. It continued in the eastern Mediterranean for hundreds and hundreds of years after that. As you've just said yourself, Darrell, it went on lifetime after lifetime. People lived their entire lives in the Byzantine Empire, and their great-grandchildren lived their entire lives in the Byzantine Empire and *their* great-grandchildren lived their entire lives in the Byzantine Empire, until finally Constantinople fell to the Turks. It was only really when Constantinople fell to the Turks that the ancient world came to an end.

Q: One historical footnote: I hadn't realized that the Byzantines used much Latin after about the reign of Heraclius in the early 7th century, when most of the remaining Latin-speaking provinces were overrun by the Avars. Didn't the Empire shift mostly to medieval Greek at that point?

Wolfe: It did. The empire that was supposed to be the Eastern Roman Empire was much more of a Greek empire than it was a Roman one, but Latin continued to be used in various esoteric disciplines. It was not the tongue of the ordinary man, nor was it the common tongue of the court, but it did continue, and it was written by scholars, and it progressed—if you want to call it progress—and changed, or it was corrupted—if you want to call it corruption—under the pens of those scholars.

Q: Would you ever follow the Byzantine model further and have an event like the battle of Manzikert? After that Byzantium collapsed relatively fast—it only took another four hundred years.

Wolfe: I wouldn't have an event like that. The possibility of that sort of event has been pre-empted by the things that take place within **The Urth of the New Sun.**

Q: By way of your interest in the classical world, could you give us some of the background for **Soldier of the Mist**? I've just started reading that. My first thought is that I vaguely remember an amnesiac character in **The Iliad**—

Wolfe: Oh. Boy. I've forgotten him, whoever it was. That's something I should be able to answer, but I can't. As for **Soldier of the Mist,** it is laid at the tail-end of the Persian Wars, and in the years just before what we consider the real classical period of Greece. Let's see, we're in 479 B.C. in the book, and I think that Socrates will be born about 475 B.C. or some such date. Of course Pericles is not around and people like Plato and Aristotle are not around. But this is the society that laid the groundwork for the classical age. The book starts with the battle of Platea, which was the last, decisive land battle of the Persian Wars. It came a year after Salamis, which was the decisive sea battle, in which Persia lost control of the sea lanes. Losing control of the sea lanes meant that the Persians could no longer maintain the enormous army with which they had invaded Greece. Herodotus says it was three million men. Most historians think that was an error. The actual number was something like three to four hundred thousand. Whoever is right—for that period, a force of even three hundred thousand men was an *immense* army. The Greeks were accustomed to dealing with hundreds or even thousands of soldiers, and when we're talking three *hundred* thousand we're talking something that was almost *unimaginable* to the Greeks of that period.

Q: The unimaginable part would be how they would feed them.

Wolfe: That was the problem with the loss of the sea lanes. As long as the Persians had control of the eastern Mediterranean, which they did up until the battle of Salamis, they fed them by shipping grain from Egypt and other parts of the Persian Empire; it was possible to supply an army of that size. After the battle of Salamis, most of the soldiers had to be pulled back into the Persian Empire, because you couldn't maintain an army like that. Such an army could not live off the land in a country like Thrace or northern Greece or Boeotia or any of those places. They didn't have that kind of a food supply. So, the Persian army was cut down to a size that was reasonable by Greek standards—let's say, thirty or forty thousand men—and that could live off the land. Of course the Persians still had hopes of defeating the Greeks, the Greeks in this case being the combined armies of Athens and Sparta, with their various satellite states. The battle of Platea was their big chance to do it, and they lost the battle. That, for practical purposes, ended the Persian Wars. But you have to understand that neither the Greeks nor the Persians knew that the war was over. It was only with hindsight that we can look back and say, "Well that was the end of the Persian Wars for all practical purposes." The Persians expected to invade Greece again with another army when they got things built up again. The Greeks expected to be invaded again.

Q: But you've made the whole setting magical, not only because the hero can see the gods, but because you don't ever call Athens and Sparta by the names Athens and Sparta. So it has a very remote feel, almost of an imaginary world. Could you explain the derivation of the names and how they're used?

Wolfe: As for how they're used, that's no great puzzle. Latro calls Athens Thought because that's what he thinks it means. As it turns out, he's right. That *is* what it means, although his derivation of it is incorrect. He's connecting Athens with *athanatos*, which anybody with a superficial knowledge of Greek would do—immortal. What's immortal is thought. *Concept* is immortal. Earth may be destroyed, but five times three is always going to be fifteen. That is truly immortal. That's what continues, that thought and many others. Latro also thinks that Sparta means *rope*, because there is a very common Greek word, *spartos*, which is rope, cord, string. Now Sparta did not mean *rope*. What it actually meant was *scattered*. But it took its name from a Greek word that was obsolete by the time Latro was in Greece. Sparta was one of those places that grew up from more than one center. Sparta was originally four villages, and these four villages became the four quarters of the city. And for a long, long time, each village maintained a separate market. Each village had its own agora. Now to a Greek who had been to Megeira and Argos and Olympia and various other Greek cities, this was unheard of. Every Greek city had a central market where people bought and sold and argued politics, and he got to Sparta and discovered that it wasn't that way there at all. There were these four shopping centers around the city. That was what impressed visitors, and that was apparently how the city got its name originally.

As far as the magical end of the novel, that is the way the people of that time saw it. If you read their writings, if you look at their world with their worldview, you will find all this magical stuff right there. You should read Herodotus on the battle of Marathon and all the supernatural occurrences that took place during the battle—the vision of the giant, and so on. Now we *know* that none of that stuff took place, but the Greece of the 5th century B.C. did not know that that stuff did not take place. They knew just the opposite. They knew that it *did*. They knew that when Apollo was really mad, it rained blood, because there was a time when Apollo was really mad and they found blood on all the rooftops in Athens. How it got there, I don't know. Some people think that someone was going around cutting the throats of chickens to panic the populace. But there was blood on the rooftops. And this was what the average man in the street saw. This was the world that he lived in.

These people gave enormous respect to the oracle at Delphi, because they honestly believed that the oracle at Delphi was a pipeline to the god Apollo. If you read their writings, there were just *miraculous* predictions coming out of Delphi. It was marvellous stuff. Maybe it was faked. Maybe it was written after the fact, but that was their thought, that was the mental world they lived in; and I'm not sure that that mental world is necessarily inferior to our rationalist world. Yes, they were certainly duped in some instances. I don't have any question of it. I think that we in our rationalist world are duped in different ways, but we're still duped occasionally. I dislike the tendency to look down on these people because they were making a different set of mistakes than we make. They made their mistakes with much more justification, because they had much less data to work on than we do, and they generally made those mistakes with a better intellect and a better heart than we seem to have.

Q: They didn't reject data as many people do today. We have science now, but *this* is the golden age of sorcery and fortune -telling. There are probably more sorcerers and fortune-tellers alive today than ever before.

Wolfe: There are probably are, not in a per-capita sense, but in a broad sense. Of course in *Soldier of the Mist,* I show one of these itinerant charlatans. He's one of the characters, Eurocles the Necromancer. As frequently happens, quite frankly, to people who get involved in charlatanism, he finds himself mixed up in supernatural activities that are outside his control and are the sort of things that he has been faking and hinting at most of his life. Now he finds himself really caught up in them and destroyed by them.

Q: By way of charlatans of classical Antiquity, have you read Lucian of Samosata's "Alexander the Quack Prophet"?

Wolfe: I have read excerpts of it. I have not read the entire work. I've read it quoted in other books.

Q: Did you have it in mind?

Wolfe: Yes, I did, and there was an actual Eurocles the Necromancer, who shows up in the court records of Athens, and I had him even more in mind.

Q: What sort of background do you have in these matters? Do you read Classical Greek?

Wolfe: "Read" is not the word. I sort of thrash my way through it. When I started this book, I didn't get very far into it before I realized that I was going to have to have some actual, solid Greek and I had none. I thought I knew a lot about the ancient world, and I found that I really had very superficial ideas and knowledge of it. So I started studying Greek. At this time—this sounds silly, I suppose, or supernatural, if you believe that Somebody looks after writers—a teacher of Classical Greek moved into the house across the street. And I went over to her and said, "I understand you're a teacher of Classical Greek. I'd like to take private lessons." I took private lesson from her at $15.00 an hour for, oh, eight months. Her name was Anne McCauslin.

Q: This is a lot more effort than most people go through to write a novel.

Wolfe: Well, you've got to do that if you're going to do the ancient world and do it *right*. Otherwise you find yourself sticking in things that you think ought to be there. I was very tempted to put in sundials, because I thought that the ancient Greeks of that period would have invented the sundial. And, by God, they hadn't. *They didn't have it.* That's all. It wasn't there then. It was probably over in Babylon. I would be amazed to learn that it wasn't in Babylon, but it wasn't in places like Athens and Sparta and Thebes. They had, as strange as it sounds to us, no regular mechanical way of dividing the day. They divided it by the activities that normally went on at a certain hour.

Q: Therefore, precisely *because* there are supernatural elements in *Soldier of the Mist,* it is a strictly realistic novel written from the viewpoint of the 5th century B.C.

Wolfe: Absolutely. When the Persians were going to land at Marathon, the Athenians sent a runner to Sparta to ask Spartan military help. The runner was a professional—these were people you hired to run messages, because that was the fastest way to get a message from Athens to Sparta—and he ran into the Peleponese and across Arcadia and delivered the message. And he got the Spartan reply, which was that they couldn't march until the festival celebrating the full of the moon, and he ran back to Athens with that message. When he reported to the Assembly, he told them that he had encountered the god Pan on the road, and he recounted his conversation with the god Pan.

Q: Presumably everyone did not regard that as particularly extraordinary.

Wolfe: They did not. These were people who, when the Persian navy was in a bad position, were sacrificing to Boreas to get him to destroy that part of the Persian navy. And he did. The north wind came down and the Persian ships were driven onto the rocks. There was a whole lot of that. There is a period, interestingly, before the battle of Platea really started, where the two armies were facing off. If you understand the strategic situation, you'll see that it was going to be pretty bad for either army to advance. The ideal thing from the Greek standpoint was for the Persians to attack *them* in their present position. The ideal thing from the Persian standpoint was for the Greeks to attack *them* in *their* present position, because the Persians are down on the plain, and the Persians have cavalry, and the Greeks are up in the hills, and they *don't*. They have very little cavalry comparatively. So each of them wants to fight where they are. So each commander has his own mantis, his own wizard, who is sacrificing and reading the portents and telling what the gods say. In all cases, the gods say, "Stay where you are. Don't attack." Then the Greeks started getting more reinforcements, and the Persian mantis said, "Now's the time to attack," and the Persian army attacked.

Q: I have a theory about this, not about the battle but about the ancient world, which is that if a time-traveler went back and tried to explain to those people scientific rationalism and a completely mechanistic universe which preludes the supernatural, he would not be understood. It would be incomprehensible nonsense.

Wolfe: It would depend on who he is talking to. If he is talking to the average man on the street in Athens, I agree with you completely. It would have been. If you were talking to the sophists, the better educated class, you would be understood. You probably, at that time, simply would not be believed. For example, at this time, the Greeks were being exposed to Persian monotheism, and they had heard it and they understood it; they just didn't believe it. They said, obviously there was the river. You could *see* the damn river, and clearly the river had a god because it acted all the time as if it had a mind of its own. It got mad and it flooded the city. It liked people and it watered their crops. It did all these things as if it were controlled by its own genius. That was good enough for them. They believed in the genius. Besides, every once in a while somebody saw him.

Q: What I was getting as was that it wouldn't be possible to be an atheist at that time.

Wolfe: I think it would be. I don't think you have to go much later than that to find some people who were getting awfully close to it. But certainly not in popular belief. Never in popular belief, not to this day in Greece. The individual, yes. We're getting very close to the sort of thing that Socrates was killed for. Athens was in big, big trouble in the Peleponesian War and

Socrates was going around saying things that a lot of people considered blasphemous. They thought that they'd better put this man to death. He could quite easily have saved himself. Of course he didn't choose to do so.

Q: Could you say something about the sequel to **Soldier of the Mist**? I gather it's a two-volume work.

Wolfe: Well, no. I am hoping to do an open-ended series here. It's a two-volume work only in the sense that I have signed a contract for a second volume. But if people like the books, I'm hoping there will be a third volume and a fourth, because I've fallen in love with the ancient world, and I would like to move Latro around in it. In the next book, I'm hoping to take him to Delphi, which you haven't seen in *Soldier of the Mist,* and I'm hoping to show him the Pythic Games, which will take place in 478 B.C. The ancient Greeks not only had the Olympics every four years; they had other games that fell in the years between. There was always a major set of games dedicated to some important god falling in the dry season of each year, when people could sleep out in the fields without getting rained on and catching cold. In 478 B.C., this would be the Pythic Games, which were held at Delphi and dedicated to Apollo, as opposed to the Olympics which were dedicated to Zeus and held at Olympia. They had the same type of events: boxing, wrestling, javelin-throwing, horse-racing, chariot-racing, lots of foot races of various lengths, and so on.

Q: What else are you working on these days?

Wolfe: I've turned in a book called *There Are Doors,* which is about a department store clerk in our world who falls in love with a visiting goddess from another universe. The visiting goddess is working as his psychiatrist's receptionist for reasons of her own, and she meets this man and lives with him briefly, and then departs, and leaves him with the warning that there are doors between his world and hers and he may find himself accidentally slipping through one of these doors. She tells him how to reverse the situation and get back to his own world.

As you've already guessed, he does indeed slip into her world and he decides he doesn't want to stop and reverse the situation. What he wants to do is find the woman that he loves, whom he knows as Laura Morgan. So he goes hunting for her, gets into various difficulties, has various adventures, acquires a cybernetic doll that was modeled on her a few years back, and by accident finds himself back in his own world after seeing something of hers, which is in many ways the same as ours, and in many ways quite different. The key thing about it that causes the difference is that in her world human males die after intercourse, just as male salmon do, and males of many species of lower animals, which means that the only forty-year-old men, for example, are men who have never had intercourse with women, and women who have children are all widows before the first child is born. The women hold the semen and may have anywhere from three or four to twenty-five children in a lifetime, all from the single experience of intercourse with her mate. For example, queen bees mate once with the drone and produce bees and bees and bees. That's what's going on in her world. Of course this is why she has gone to his world, because she doesn't like the idea of killing the man because he has been her lover.

It gave me a chance to explore a little bit what such a world would be like. For example, a number of wars that have taken place in our world, the American Civil War and the First World War, for examples, have not taken place in her world, because there is a shortage of young men and there is a much greater sense of the value of young men since they will die very shortly if they do reproduce the human race. And of course there are people who are trying to dodge around the biological facts in various ways. Eventually, he does reconnect with the goddess.

Q: How are the Feminist critics going to take this?

Wolfe: I think that's going to be interesting, but if I get anything but straight hostility I'll be delighted. What I've gotten from Feminist critics has been, by and large, straight hostility to whatever I've written. But I think that feminist critics, like other critics whose orientation is primarily political one way or another, Marxist or whatever, are looking for someone who will write their party line. And I'm not going to do that. I'm not a party-line writer, not for them, not for the Marxists, not for a lot of other people. I am writing the story line, not the party line. I write it the way I think it should be written. In the goddess's universe, obviously the president is a woman. Many, though not all, high officials are women, because very few men live past their twenties.

Q: Well, I'm looking forward to the book in any case. Thank you, Gene.

JANE YOLEN

Q: So, how about this Harry Potter kid? How do you as a children's fantasist feel seeing something in your field suddenly take off into the stratosphere? Is there something particularly about this particular time that makes it right for fantasy for children, or are ALL times right for children's fantasy? (I might suggest the latter myself, and that the variable is whether or not the parents allow it.)

Yolen: This is of course a series of questions all children's fantasists are being asked these days. For me it is a particularly thorny question as I published a novel called *Wizard's Hall* eight years before the first Harry Potter book. In it a boy named Henry goes off to a wizard's academy though he doesn't think he has any talent. He has a smudgy nose and fly-away hair. At the Hall he is given a bedroom with stars in the ceiling. Pictures of the teachers hang on the wall, and the pictures talk and smile and move. There is a wicked wizard who used to be associated with the school who is trying to destroy it and the teachers. Henry, of course, becomes the one who saves the day. No quidditch game, though.

So I am a bit thorny on the issue of Harry Potter. Why is Harry such a phenom? Well, that is the billion dollar question. And if any of us could answer it, we'd do it ourselves. Certainly the books are not as well written as—say—Diana Wynne Jones or Philip Pullman's British fantasies. Maybe that's one of the reasons. The Potter books are easy to access. They are fantasy fast food. They have a very cinematic feel to them (and easily translated to the screen without missing a beat evidently—I have not seen the movie yet, though I have read the books.) And Jo Rowling had a wonderful backstory—broke single mom on the dole writing in a coffee-shop in Edinburgh. It made for great interviews and news stories once the book got started.

It's interesting to note that the first book (like Madeleine L'Engle's *A Wrinkle in Time*) went to every large publisher in the country of origin before a smaller publisher brought it out. Again—great backstory for publicity.

But a phenomenon makes its own rules. And breaks them as well.

Q: What is special about writing fantasy for children? How does it differ from writing for adults?

Yolen: Facetious answer: small children, talking animals, fewer words, and no sex scenes.

Facetious answer number two: lots of ardent fans for life who send wonderful hand-written letters enclosing their school photos.

Facetious answer number three: Books remain on the shelves and in school libraries forever.

There's a certain amount of truth in all three of those answers. But I suspect the real answer is: I write what I want to read myself. I write what comes out. I am more a short form person (I began as a poet) than a long former. Which makes a children's novel—the Harry Potter books and *The Golden Compass* notwithstanding)—the perfect size for me. And I also suspect that I have the brain of a precocious nine year old.

Q: Do you think children prefer fantasy to realism? Why?

Yolen: I think for younger children the line between fantasy and realism is thin at best. Think invisible friends, tea parties with dolls, major battles with GI Joes. Even children grades 3-6: think cops and robbers with stick guns, think playing Camelot/Harry Potter/Lord of the Rings/Star Wars/ etc. They certainly prefer reading fantasy to realism, if you look at book sale figures. Of course that has to include all the talking animal stories, fairy tales, and takeoffs (Captain Underpants, for example) as well as straight forward high fantasy.

Q: Many fantasists insist they write fantasy because that enables them to write about true and important things, rather than the trivia required in some areas of mainstream realism. Is this your take on it?

Yolen: Fantasy writing has to be as precise as any kind of writing—and perhaps more so—since the world invented has to be as real as the everyday. So I think rather the opposite is true. What makes a good fantasy is that the True and Important Things (as some children's fantasy would have it) have to be embedded within a real framework, though the framework encases magical or fantastical settings/creatures/spells rather than the mundane.

Q: I've also heard it claimed that you have to write more honestly for children, because they won't tolerate evasions and obfuscations. Is this so?

Yolen: I have never gotten a letter from an adult that says, "You are my second favorite author." Or "I think you could have had a better ending on your book." Or "I thought the beginning of your book was slow and didn't understand it all the way through." But I have gotten such things from kids.

So it may be that adults are less honest in their face-to-face critiques. Or perhaps it's because children are often assigned to write to authors in school.

Certainly it's true that half-baked or not-entirely clear ideas get a real working over by the kids. They want to know WHY WHY WHY. They cannot be fobbed off with, "Well, that's just the way I wrote it." They live inside a book more than most adult readers. Diana Wynne Jones has written extensively and cleverly about this.

Q: I wonder if the reason kids live more intensely with a book is that by the time they've grown up, they've been told that "imaginary" things are frivolous. You can see this in mainstream criticism, which is deeply suspicious of the imagination. I call this the Protestant Work Ethic of Literature, the idea that if you enjoy a work it is foolish and probably wicked, and that "real" literature only consists of "real" subject matter.

Any thoughts? Is the rise of fantasy perhaps attributed to the failure of this ideology from the '60s onwards?

Yolen: Actually, I think that kids who adore fantasy (as opposed to those who read Harry Potter because it the Big Fad of the Year) are still reading fantasy as adults. But once most kids get into high school, they read a lot less—this has been documented. Being a big reader suddenly takes on a nerd/jerk connotation. Peer power sorts out readers, much like that hat in Harry Potter.

Q: Meanwhile, let's discuss how you got into writing fantasy. When did you start writing, and did you write fantasy from the start? Am I correct that you didn't start out fresh from school as a writer, but came to it a little later in life? So what did you do first?

Yolen: I have been a writer all my life. My parents were both writers, my father a journalist, my mother a short story writer and creator of crossword puzzles and double acrostics. Most of their friends were well-known writers (like James Thurber and Cornelius Ryan and Will Oursler.) My father was president of the Overseas Press Club for a while. In fact, when I was young, I thought ALL grown-ups were writers, that after their day jobs (policeman, fireman, teacher, pediatrician, butcher) they went home and spent the evenings writing. But what I wrote was nonfiction, journalism—and poetry. I thought fiction writers were gods. (Well, now I know better.)

My fiction career started in 1963 when I sold a couple of children's picture book fairy tales. The first book I sold though, (when I was 22) was non fiction, about women pirates, called *Pirates in Petticoats*. The second book I sold was in rhyme. It was only when I got to my third and fourth books (at 23)—those fairy tale books—that I was really off and running. It was years, though, before I wrote an adult book. Short was my mode. Poetry, fairy tales, children's novels. Then I started getting some of my more sophisticated fairy tales into *F&SF*. Ed Ferman loved my work, had no idea I had about fifteen or twenty books out (including a National Book Award nominee) because he knew nothing about children's books. I sent him a story after reading a redacted Irish fairy tale in *F&SF* by Greg Frost, and thinking, "Hey—that's what I do." Ed bought it because he loved it, not because he had a clue as to my reputation. So for a number of years I wrote stories for F&SF that were then packaged together in children's book collections. And that was my only connection to the world of adult f&sf

until I wrote two short stories for Terri Windling anthologies, both about this strange world where grieving was the highest art form. It metamorphosed after that into a novel, *Cards of Grief*, which Terri Windling edited for Tor. My first adult novel. But not my last.

Q: A lot of your "children's books" can be readily enjoyed by adults, and, as you said, your work fit into *F&SF* without a ripple, so what is the real difference between a children's story and an adult story? That is, a story for older children. The differences in vocabulary and paragraph length are obvious enough in a book for very young children, but isn't much of the rest marketing? Your fairy tales, for instance, are published in *F&SF*, and then are collected in, say, *The Hundredth Dove*, which looks like a children's book to me.

And where does *Tales of Wonder* go in the library, in the children's section or the adult?

Yolen: It is all marketing. Think about it—was *Jonathan Freaking Seagull* a children's book or an adult book? *Watership Down? The Amber Spyglass? Harry Potter and the Sorcerer's Stone?* I read Thomas Mann's *Joseph in Egypt* when I was ten and *War and Peace* when I was 15. Children's books as a particular publishing niche goes back to the 19teens, and YA books were invented in the 1960s. Before that were books that found their own audiences. And many books—especially fantasy and fairy tales—cross over whatever marketing line the publishers draw in the sand. Speaking of my own books, *The Hundredth Dove* was published as a children's book, *Tales of Wonder* and *Briar Rose* and *Sister Emily's Lightship* as adult books. However a number of the stories from *Dove* were in *F&SF,* a number of stories in *Tales* and *Sister Emily* were first published as children's stories, and *Briar Rose* is now being brought out with a new cover as a YA book. All marketing.

Q: Marketing yes, but I think you must admit it is not the ordinary ten-year-old than would read Thomas Mann's *Joseph in Egypt* or an ordinary 15-year-old who reads *War and Peace*.

It's got to be more than just marketing. There are indeed many books which can cross over, and others which were once published for adults but which have since become "children's literature" (Robert Louis Stevenson, Alexander Dumas, Jules

Verne), but if someone were to try to do a children's edition of, say, *Ulysses* by James Joyce, or *Gravity's Rainbow* by Thomas Pynchon, this would not work.

So isn't a children's book recognizable, at least in the broadest sense, by content?

Yolen: Only in the broadest sense. There are YAs that are more full of sex and sadism than any Russian novel I studied in college. There are picture books about celebrating Chanukah in a concentration camp, about the bomb falling on Hiroshima and its aftermath, about the death of the zoo elephants in wartime Japan, about a Taino child during and after Columbus' visit. . .and these are artfully disguised as fully illustrated books for children. (And only one of them written by me!)

In that broadest sense, a children's book is what a children's book department publishes. Also in the broadest sense, a children's book is what children read. So they may no longer be reading *The Wind in the Willows* because it's too old-fashioned, and it perforce becomes an adult book. But they may be reading Tolkien (which was published for adults) because they saw the movie. The smart publisher finds ways to maximize these changes in taste. You and I can call one a children's book and the other an adult book all we want, but the market (and marketing department) will outfox us.

Q: An awful lot of people forget what it was like to be a child by the time they're twenty, it seems. How is it that a writer, some decades removed, can still write so convincing about children and from a child's viewpoint?

Yolen: Some of us never leave childhood. I think Maurice Sendak, Bruce Coville, Paula Danziger among others have a direct connection to their child id. I on the other hand do not remember my childhood at all and so am forced to create it afresh. My dis-memory does not come from a miserable childhood. It was quite an easy, comfortable childhood. I simply don't remember anything but a few snapshots of my life before high school. Strange that. And some who write for children (like some who write for adults) do so by tapping in on fads, trends, movies, pop culture. They profit well by it. It's not my kind of writing but it's certainly all around us.

Q: So, what are children convinced by? Something which is congruent to their lives, or something which assumes an emotional reality of its own even if it is beyond experience?

Yolen: You know, if I could answer THAT question, I'd be a millionaire. So would every children's book author and illustrator and publishing companies would be rolling in dough. I mean—who really knows? Sometimes a child loves a book because it has her favorite color, or his name is the same as the hero's. I remember what first drew me to *Mary Poppins* wasn't the magic, but that one of the Banks children was named Jane.

Q: Would you explain what you mean by the striking phrase (picked up from your essays and from the earlier interview I did with you about 20 years ago), "pornography of innocence?"

Yolen: I meant that there are things in children's books that we feel we have so outgrown as adults, that they are embarrassments. That we distance ourselves from them as we would pornography. Notions of truth, good/evil, loyalty etc.

Q: How do you deal with attempts to censor children's books? I have the impression that this is the real front line for freedom of expression these days. Just about anything goes in adult books. Is this so?

Yolen: I have had children's books banned, hidden behind library desks, front covers torn off. And my adult book *Briar Rose* that is now being brought out by Tor as a YA book, was burned on the steps of the Board of Education in Kansas City. It has less to do with freedom of expression than freedom of idiocy to take over our schools and libraries. We give more power to those who would ban books than those who would share books. I have known teachers who lost their jobs over using books—award-winning books—in their classrooms.

Q: What are you working on these days, for children and for adults?

Yolen: For kids the following are coming out this spring: *Hippolyta and the Curse of the Amazons,* a middle grade novel (HarperCollins); *The Bagpiper's Ghost*, a middle grade novel (Harcourt); *Firebird,* a picture book (HarperCollins); *Wild Wings*, picture book (Boyds Mills).

I am revising a major YA Arthurian novel called *Sword of the Rightful King*, writing a mythological middle grade novel with my friend Bob Harris called *Jason and the Gorgon's Blood,* writing a middle grade horror novel with my son Adam Stemple and based on a modern version of Pied Piper of Hamelin, working on a cookbook with my daughter Heidi Stemple, a new book of poems with my son Jason Stemple the photographer.

I have no plans for an adult book right now.

Q: Thanks, Jane.

GEORGE ZEBROWSKI

Q: Rather than the usual opening, let's start this with a State of Zebrowski report. Where do you see your career right now? Where do you think you fit into the field?

Zebrowski: I never think about fitting into the field. I write what I want to write, and feel that it may be of interest to someone who wishes to read over my shoulder. Currently I am finishing *Cave of Stars,* for HarperPrism, a companion to *Macrolife.* A new novel, *Brute Orbits,* is just out from the same publisher. There will very likely be reissues of *Macrolife,* and *Stranger Suns.* I have a major anthology about space colonies, *Skylife,* co-edited with Gregory Benford, set for mid-1999 publication from Harcourt, and plans for three new novels and a story collection. After having a tough time in the early '90s, I think I have landed on my feet and am going forward.

Q: You're doing a lot better than a lot of people whose careers seem to have stopped with the demise of the midlist, or the takeover of the midlist by media fiction. Do you consider yourself more fortunate than most?

Zebrowski: I never gave up, and many good people stood by me and helped. But the media have not left me untouched. I have written two *Star Trek* novels with Pamela Sargent, and I am surprised at how much I enjoyed them. But I suppose that the editor, John Ordover, a writer himself, decided he was going to go enlist more established writers to do them. I very much enjoyed writing them and don't regret them. I wouldn't want to have them continue endlessly, but there will be at least one more, *Dyson Sphere,* with Charles Pellegrino, with whom I also wrote *The Killing Star,* which was published to unanimous praise. It was an important event in my life. I never thought I would collaborate on novels with anyone, but Pellegrino—who is, by the way, the author of the "Jurassic Park recipe" for cloning dinosaurs and a scientist who works in six or seven fields, and a very, very good writer—was just irresistible. When he came along I could not turn away from working with him. He has a major novel just published called *Dust,* which Warner Brothers has already optioned for a major film. I will probably do another novel with him called *The Biotimers,* probably next year or the year after.

Q: There are a lot of people right now expressing concern over whether or not individual SF writers can survive the competition of brand-names. There are a handful of big-name writers who get share-cropped, or whose series or universes get share-cropped, and then there are all the media tie-in books, which alone, according to *Locus,* constitute 51% of the field. These make the individual writer anonymous. So how is a writer who just writes his own material to survive?

Zebrowski: I am better known than I realize. This is told to me by editors. I suppose in a field where good things can continue to happen, that should tone down anybody's complaints. But I do wonder whether good things are merely slipping through. There is no system of oppression which is perfect. There are cracks in every system, and good things get through. I hope this will continue. But the system may become tougher and meaner and drive out all individual work. The cutbacks of the '90s were not only shortsighted and ineffective in their own terms, they also blighted the lives and talents of some fifty writers. Some will not recover, but neither will the reputations of those responsible. I long to see the SF memoirs of 2020!

Q: I guess I am idealistic enough to think that individual work has an economic advantage in the long term. If you want a Gene Wolfe book or a Ray Bradbury book, you can't really hire somebody else to write one.

Zebrowski: The individual is in the position of having to create his own market, in the way that Philip José Farmer created his own demand for himself. But it took an enormous length of time. Farmer was a very well-respected writer from 1952 to 1960, but almost unpublished in book form during that time. In the '60s it was mostly original paperbacks. He never started as a young man. I think he's in his eighties now, and his greatest success has been in the past twenty years.

Q: Better late than never, or, for some writers, better early than never. I guess what you're also doing is showing the continued viability of science fiction novels which are, to put it simply, about something.

Zebrowski: To coin Blish's phrase again.

Q: Yes. The reason that someone might want to reprint *Macrolife* and they wouldn't want to reprint a totally generic book, is that *Macrolife* is about something, and has content which isn't in a dozen other books. This is what I mean by the individual writer having the economic advantage in the long run. You have something no one else does. Mere literary technicians or assembly-line workers can be replaced.

Zebrowski: With a little bit of luck. *Macrolife* is a book that simply refused to die, even in my mind, though I certainly went through periods of devaluing it in my own head. But it just never went away. Ten years after it was first published, Easton Press did a leatherbound Masterpieces edition with a long introduction by Ian Watson. That sold out completely and I am told that they may reissue it. When *Cave of Stars* comes out, the companion book—not a sequel, but a companion, which will cover a period of time mentioned briefly in Part II of *Macrolife*—there will be a paperback reissue of *Macrolife* also.

It was a very problematic book for me. I took a lot of heat for it. There were times when *I* didn't know what to make of it. It's almost twenty years old. All I can say today is that it's a book I had to write.

Q: It's a book that's been cited as continuing the tradition of Olaf Stapledon. You and I were just on a panel ((at Contradiction, 17 October 1997)) about Texts Behind the Texts. So could you describe some of the texts behind *Macrolife,* your reading of Stapledon or whatever, and how this influenced you?

Zebrowski: Stapledon and Clarke, both. The Clarkean voice is certainly present in *Macrolife*. I think I take a much more hopeful view cosmology than Stapledon does. Stapledon sees things ending. I take the view of the mathematician Kurt Goedel that we live in an open universe which will never be complete and our knowledge will never be complete. So *Macrolife* is optimistic in that sense.

One thing I should say about *Macrolife* is that at the time I wrote it, much of the cosmology, which I took for granted—they've learned since—was much more problematic and much more conjectural than it is today. There are certain cosmologists who are going way beyond what I have in even the third part of *Macrolife*. But I did not realize that what I had taken for granted was still so conjectural at the time. I thought it was much more accepted. And I think I was generally in the right direction.

Q: Isn't the key to all this writing a book which continues to have power even if the scientific ideas date? This is very obvious in Wells. The Martians *didn't* invade in 1898. A modern publisher's sales person would argue that unless you want to take *The War of the Worlds* as alternate history, the book is obsolete. No it isn't. The book has all the power it ever did.

Zebrowski: You're describing a certain hallucinatory strength in the story-telling, to the point where the reader knows all the shortcomings and all the differences, and it doesn't matter at all. *Macrolife* is a gripping dream still in my mind and obviously in the minds of some readers. Not all. But that is the secret of such a book, whether or not it has a hallucinatory strength, even if it's quite wrong. *The Time Machine* would not have taken the time traveler to the end of the world thirty million years hence. It's not any time at all, given the time-scales we're used to today in modern cosmology.

Q: This brings us to the contrast between hard science fiction as actual speculation, as opposed to science fiction as myth. How do you combine the two?

Zebrowski: A science-fiction story deals with the human effect of a scientific, technological, or social change. It's the human effect which makes it a work of literature. It's the changes of whatever kind that make it science fiction. I get this all from James Blish. You try to make the human effect as good a work of literature as you can, and then you try to make the speculation as plausible as you can. But if the human effect is at all powerful, the work will live even if all the science is wrong. Poul Anderson's "Call Me Joe" is certainly not set on Jupiter, but there might somewhere in the universe be a planet like the Jupiter of "Call Me Joe." You don't care that this Jupiter is not the one.

Q: It seems to me that there is an extra-literary virtue in some science fiction, in the sense that a novel about colonizing the Moon could contain interesting ideas about what it might actually be like to colonize the Moon or how this could be achieved, a real matter which has nothing to do with literature. This aspect could be present quite apart from any literary merit. These two parts of the book could age differently.

Zebrowski: I am afraid I look down upon novels that have just the speculative element and do not succeed as novels also. I would like to have it all. If I've been working toward anything at all in my career, it's toward that fusion.

Q: Do you have a sense then that you are writing a more difficult kind of science fiction, because you have to do it all? Satire, for instance, can just exaggerate things for effect, without the need to realistically explain how the exaggerations in the novel could be so.

Zebrowski: My good friend James Morrow writes a kind of satirical SF which is by any stretch of the imagination fantasy. But he works it out in Campbellian fashion. Once you have assumed the fantastic element, everything is realistically worked out as if it were an *Analog* story. He brings also to that a novelist's skill at least on the order of Kurt Vonnegut, and a great wit. I would like to be able to do it all. I work toward doing it all. Is it hard? It's enormously hard. I think to write an even decently bad novel is hard. To write a good one is very hard. To write with brilliance the kind of science fiction I am describing is nearly impossible. To speculate realistically about the future in a way that will keep you current a hundred years from now? Probably not doable at all. I think it was Greg Bear who was saying to me once that he would like to write a science-fiction novel in the Stapledonian fashion, as just a history, with no concession to entertainment or to novels, and just speculate straight-out. If you tried to do that in a novel, I think he said to me, it would be incomprehensible to most readers. And if you tried to be realistic, taking into account everything that we know about the universe, cosmology, physics, whatever, it would be impossible for most readers to understand. You'd have to do the equivalent of explaining a bicycle or an automobile or a water-faucet at every step, as in a contemporary story.

Still, I think this kind of science fiction can glimpse possible future in some small measure. Whether any writer can actually do it all at the level of genius, I don't know. I think we have to keep trying.

Q: Who do you think has come closest?

Zebrowski: I look around at my colleagues. Gregory Benford and Greg Bear are certainly outstanding examples of this melding of literary virtues and hard-SF enterprise. There are many good writers around, Michael Bishop, Pamela Sargent, Howard Waldrop, Jack Dann, all working at a high level of literary skill. All of us are, to some extent, falling behind in the thought aspect of science fiction, because it requires an enormous amount of continuing education to keep up with everything. So what actually gets into SF novels, even the best ones, is what is easily digested and easily handled. Then other writers will pick it up and digest it even further.

To use unpredigested ideas which are fresh, which come from reading the raw materials of what's going on in the sciences today, is an enormous task. Writing a mystery novel drawn entirely out of your own head and experience, without doing any research to speak of, seems like a relief. I have a mystery novel that I wanted to write, and I know I would be able to write it with the kind of ease and control that comes from being entirely in control of the material, whereas with the most ambitious science fiction, you constantly get the feeling that no matter how brilliant you may be, you are beneath the material. You're trying to reach up to it and grasp it. You feel like Odd John's biographer in Olaf Stapledon's *Odd John*. You're never going to penetrate that opaque mask of the superman.

Q: If you can't keep on the cutting edge of astrophysics and number theory and anthropology and number theory and neurobiology, etc.—and obviously you can't—so doesn't this suggest that the science fiction writer needs to specialize?

Zebrowski: Look at Poul Anderson in his recent books, beginning with *The Boat of a Million Years,* and also with *Harvest of Stars, The Stars Are Also Fire,* and others. He has managed in these volumes to speculate on a variety of subjects and developments. I find it remarkable that a writer who—well, I shouldn't find it remarkable; he has been writing for such a long time and been interested in so much that somehow it's all come together for him. That he was able to meld it all into a story *is* remarkable.

Usually you come across a new scientific idea or technical development, and the first thing you struggle with is how to make a story out of it. The bald stating of the idea is not going to give it to you. This is increasingly evident when you try to write a story set millions of years in the future. A story like *The City and the Stars* is today a hundred times more difficult, if you want to take into account everything we know about deep time. I've been writing a story, maybe a novella, or it may turn into a novel, called "After the Stars Are Gone," and it's going to be my *Against the Fall of Night.* What I have come up with are story-structures, story-arcs, that I feel have almost been given to me as a gift from God knows where—and I don't believe in God. I've discussed the story with others and one fellow writer said to me, "You've actually come up with a plot point that no one has ever come up with." So it might actually work out.

I think you have to come up to the wall of hard SF, stand with your nose against it long enough to start seeing the cracks in it—and then you go through to see how it must be done.

Q: I can also see this kind of "deep time" science fiction partaking of a line of development which is more myth than science. *Against the Fall of Night,* for instance, has its roots in the last pages of *The Time Machine,* and extends through *The Night Land* and probably the Zothique cycle. This is a development which is still continuing. Gene Wolfe has contributed to it admirably in *The Book of the New Sun.*

Zebrowski: Some years ago I said that the generation starship was far from through. Then Gene Wolfe comes across with his four generation-starship novels, his Long Sun books, and I said, "Aha! Somebody has been thinking along similar lines." Almost anything can be looked at again and freshened if you have an inquisitive mind and you have the literary skills to carry it through. I think *Against the Fall of Night* was, by today's standards, a fairly easy story for Clarke to write. He wrote it at the beginning of his career. It's a lyrical, musical work. He says that his influence was "The Afternoon of a Faun" by Debussy, a piece of music. Compare it to Gregory Benford's companion to *Against the Fall of Night, Beyond the Fall of Night,* and you see how times have changed. I'm going to try it my way, if the marketplace gives me a chance. It's not even contracted for. It's just something I am doing on the side. But I think I have some originality with the ideas I am working with that can only be gotten, to repeat myself, by coming up to the blank wall, the blank wall being how to treat these cosmological ideas. It's a matter of being there imaginatively, until it becomes obvious to you how to do it. You have to have patience.

Q: I think there's a difference between an actual idea and a trope. As an example of something that's more a trope than an idea, would it would be possible to write a fresh Lost Race novel today?

Zebrowski: I think so. In fact, at one point I had an idea for a novel called *Under New York.* New York sinks away under the ground, and three hundred years later it's like a lost generation-starship. People have managed to survive, so you have Fifth Avenue under a big rock, and street lights. A whole culture, a very small group of people, has managed to continue to live there. You could, if you developed enough of the history of New York and enough of the sociology, develop a story. You wouldn't tell the reader what has happened on the surface that has prevented these people from ever being rescued or has prevented them from coming up to the surface. The regionalism of setting it in a sunken New York is what would make the book.

Q: It would be like the classic Lost Race novel, about the explorer from the outside coming in and discovering the lost world of New York.

Zebrowski: You could do it any number of ways. That would be one. Or the people there could develop an interest in what's topside and perhaps run into an explorer coming down.

Q: Actually Whitley Strieber's *The Wolfen* is ultimately a Lost Race novel. It's about a hidden culture of werewolves in New York.

Zebrowski: I've not read it. But anything can be done again if you take a fresh perspective on it, and a fresh perspective can be done if you take a vehement, trenchant approach. But genuine originality is a much greater goal.

Q: In other words, you have to think in terms of something beyond how long this will pay the grocery bills. One has to actually care about what you're writing.

Zebrowski: You have to fall in love with it until the damn thing sings to you.

Q: I think the real key for writers is this: Suppose you are independently wealthy, so that you will live in secure luxury for the rest of your life, your children will be provided for in a like manner, and so on. But a condition of this wealth is that you may write what you want, and it will be published, but you won't be paid. Then, would you keep on writing?

Zebrowski: This is exactly what I am planning . . . [Laughs.] But if you look back on a typical science fiction writer's career, and you count the personal cost and the payment, we have all of us in one way or another given it away.

Q: You mean given away the fruits of your labor?

Zebrowski: Yes, because I don't think that the lifetime that has made me a writer has been paid for in any of the money I have earned as a writer. It would probably come out as a deficit, no matter what sums were paid..

Q: But it's been paid for by the fact that you're a writer rather than a shoe salesman.

Zebrowski: It's been worth it to me, but not in monetary terms.

Q: There is something far more than money involved here. As a writer you can point to something you have done, as opposed to merely your check stubs.

Zebrowski: Yes, this is so easily forgotten.

Q: In the context of all this, one hears a lot of gloomy things from writers about how the hard science novel is an endangered species and the midlist is disappearing. But you seem to have a more optimistic view of your ability to continue doing all this.

Zebrowski: I wouldn't say that. I would say that the battle is joined. That's what life is for, to stand up for what you think you should do. I can't say it hasn't been difficult. It has been enormously difficult. Am I optimistic? Things are pretty bad. But I have a thing called Zebrowski's Law. The good happens along with the bad. There's a lot of bad, but you have to be there to oppose it at every step. When you go down, there have to be others to take up the position. It's the only way. But in order to get anywhere and overcome any difficulty, you have to recognize how bad things are. At every step in my career, when I have complained, that complaint could have been left as a complaint, or something could have been done about it.

Q: But ultimately what you do about it is write indispensable, unique books.

Zebrowski: You do what you can do and hope that'll be enough. If that's not enough, you'll go down.

Q: There's a sad phenomenon in our field right now, of writers who are in a post-novelist phase, often very respected ones, whose books have been pushed out of the midlist, so they can sell all the short stories they want, but their novel-writing careers seem to be over. I can't name any names, lest it become a self-fulfilling prophecy. But there are writers, who have had solid, thirty-year careers in our field, who can't sell books anymore. I think the reason is precisely because they *do* have a track record. The sales force says, "This guy has a flat-line in his sales. There's no upward curve. We would do better to invest our money in a new writer who might become a best-seller in five years." So a lot of people do go down.

Zebrowski: One of the arguments I made to my publishers in the early '90s was that I had reached a stage where I had twelve or thirteen novels in outline or in draft. The number of short stories was virtually unlimited in my files. I was ready to make the next step. My argument to them was, "Are you going to help me take that next step, or are you going to stop me right here?" Luckily, as the '90s wore on, the editors and friends were there to help me take the next step.

Q: Thank you, George.

INDEX

ABOUT THE INTERVIEWEES

Peter S. Beagle (1939 —) is the author of *A Fine and Private Place, The Last Unicorn, The Folk of the Air, Tamsin,* and several more fantasy novels. He wrote the screenplay for the animated version of *The Lord of the Rings.*

Octavia Butler (1947 —) began publishing SF in 1971. She has won the Hugo and the Nebula awards. Among her notable books are *Kindred, Adulthood Rites, The Parable of the Sower,* etc.

Philip José Farmer (1918 —) is one of the truly great figures in science fiction, who made an explosive debut with his sexually explicit novella "The Lovers" in 1952. He has been pushing the boundaries of the field ever since in such works as *Flesh, Father to the Stars, A Feast Unknown,* and many more. He is perhaps best known for his Riverworld sequence, beginning with *To Your Scattered Bodies Go* (1971) in which every human being who ever lived is mysteriously resurrected along the banks of an enormous river.

Charles L. Harness (1915 —) is best known for the critically admired and surprisingly durable *The Paradox Men* (1949), one of the great classics of space opera. An omnibus of his best work is *An Ornament to His Profession,* published by NESFA. He is still active and writing, particularly for *Weird Tales.*

Michael Kandel (1941 —) is an editor at Harcourt, and perhaps best known as the *good* translator of Stanislaw Lem. He is himself a writer of satirical SF novels, including *Strange Invasions, In Between Dragons, Captain Jack Zodiac*, and *Panda Ray*.

R.A. Lafferty (1914-2002) was one of the great comic geniuses of science fiction. His works include *Past Master, Space Chantey, The Reefs of Earth, Archipelago, The Flame is Green, The Fall of Rome, Okla Hannali*, and many short stories, some of the best of which are collected in *Nine Hundred Grand-mothers*. He won the Hugo Award in 1973 for "Eurema's Dam."

Jack McDevitt (1935 —) made his first sale to *Twilight Zone* in 1981, although he has since become well-known for hard science fiction, such as *The Hercules Text, Moonfall, A Talent for War, Eternity Road, Omega*, etc.

Tim Powers (1952 —) began his career with two Laser books, but is much better known for historically-based fantasies, such as *The Drawing of the Dark, The Anubis Gates, Declare*, etc.

Charles Sheffield (1935-2002) was a British-born physicist long resident in the United States who began writing science fiction in the late 1970s and quickly established himself as one of the masters of hard, scientifically-accurate SF. His books include *Sight of Proteus, The Web Between the Stars, Erasmus Magister, Between the Strokes of Night*, etc. He won the Hugo and Nebula for the novelet "Georgia On My Mind." He served one term as president of the Science Fiction Writers of America.

Susan Shwartz (1949 —) has written both science fiction and fantasy, including *Byzantium's Crown, The Woman of Flowers, Shards of Empire, Cross and Crescent*, and *Silk Roads and Shadows*. She has also edited such anthologies as *Hecate's Cauldron* and *Habitats*.

Michael Swanwick (1950 —) had two of his first three published stories on the Nebula ballot. He has won numerous awards since. His works include *Vacuum Flowers, Stations of the Tide, The Iron Dragon's Daughter, Jack Faust, Bones of the Earth*, and a great many more. His short fiction regularly appears in *Asimov's SF*.

Evangeline Walton (1907-1996) published her first novel, *The Virgin and the Swine*, a retelling of a branch of the Welsh *Mabinogion* in 1936. But she remained obscure until 1970, when Lin Carter rediscovered her, publishing *The Virgin and the Swine* in the Ballantine Adult Fantasy Series as *The Island of the Mighty*. He was delighted to discover that Ms. Walton was not only still around, but had three more novels in the series, unpublished. Suddenly she was an overnight success, the books became classics of Celtic fantasy, and she give the honor due her late in life, receiving a special World Fantasy Award in 1985 and a Lifetime Achievement Award in 1989.

Gene Wolfe (1931 —) is one of the greatest living masters of both science fiction and fantasy, best-known for *The Book of the New Sun* (1980-83). His other works include *Operation Ares, The Devil in a Forest, There Are Doors, Soldier of the Mist, Soldier of Arete, Castleview, Free Live Free, Peace, The Wizard* and the four-volume *Book of the Long Sun*. He has been nominated for and won many awards, and was given the Life Achievement Award by the World Fantasy Convention in 1996.

Jane Yolen (1939 —) is a hugely prolific and hugely respected author of children's books, including many fantasies and fairy tales. Her work has long since crossed many category boundaries, much of it being published for adults, including *Briar Rose, Sister Light Sister Dark, White Jenna*, and *The Cards of Grief*.

George Zebrowski (1945 —) is a leading writer of hard/philosophical SF, including *Macrolife, Stranger Suns, Brute Orbits*, and many more. He as also been a prolific editor and anthologist.

ABOUT THE INTERVIEWER

Darrell Schweitzer (1952 —) is a fantasy (and occasionally science-fiction) writer, whose novels include *The White Isle, The Shattered Goddess,* and *The Mask of the Sorcerer.* He has published over 250 short stories, many of which are collected in *Tom O'Bedlam's Night Out, Refugees from an Imaginary Country, Nightscapes, Transients, The Great World and the Small,* etc. He has published much poetry, non-fiction, and criticism, edited anthologies, and presently is co-editor of *Weird Tales.* He did his first interview, with Gardner Dozois, in 1973.